He wondered how it would feel to kiss her…

As soon as the thought crossed his mind he dismissed it. She was a journalist…a breed he despised! They were hard-bitten—uncaring—trouble-stirring…

Isobel's heart was pounding as if she had run a long-distance marathon. She felt shaky and hot inside. And the worst thing was the feeling of pleasure that had blazed inside her just from the lightest brush of his fingertips. It had never happened to her before with anyone. And the fact that it had happened so easily, and with such a casual touch, *with Marco* was horrifying.

He was Marco Lombardi, one of the most notorious womanisers on the planet, and she couldn't afford to forget that even for a minute.

Kathryn Ross was born in Zambia, where her parents happened to live at that time. Educated in Ireland and England, she now lives in a village near Blackpool, Lancashire. Kathryn is a professional beauty therapist, but writing is her first love. As a child she wrote adventure stories, and at thirteen was editor of her school magazine. Happily, ten writing years later, DESIGNED WITH LOVE was accepted by Mills & Boon. A romantic Sagittarian, she loves travelling to exotic locations.

Recent titles by the same author:

THE MEDITERRANEAN'S WIFE BY CONTRACT
ITALIAN MARRIAGE: IN NAME ONLY

INTERVIEW
WITH A PLAYBOY

BY
KATHRYN ROSS

All the characters in this book have no existence outside the imagination of the author, and have no relation whatsoever to anyone bearing the same name or names. They are not even distantly inspired by any individual known or unknown to the author, and all the incidents are pure invention.

First published in Great Britain 2011
Harlequin Mills & Boon Limited,
Eton House, 18-24 Paradise Road, Richmond, Surrey TW9 1SR

© Kathryn Ross 2011

ISBN: 978 0 263 88635 1

Harlequin Mills & Boon policy is to use papers that are natural, renewable and recyclable products and made from wood grown in sustainable forests. The logging and manufacturing process conform to the legal environmental regulations of the country of origin.

Printed and bound in Spain
by Litografia Rosés, S.A., Barcelona

INTERVIEW WITH A PLAYBOY

CHAPTER ONE

'WELL, look who has just walked into the reception area,' Marco Lombardi murmured with a gleam of pleasure in his voice.

They'd been in the middle of studying an intensely intricate set of financial records, but his accountant looked up from the sheets of paper and curiously followed his boss's gaze towards the security monitors on the wall.

'Isn't that the reporter who has been hanging around the Sienna building for the last couple of days?' he said with a frown.

'Indeed it is.' Marco smiled. 'But don't worry, John, she's here by invitation.'

'Invitation? You mean you are *allowing* her in to see you?'

'You could say that,' Marco replied, somewhat amused by the other man's astonished tone.

'But you hate the press—you never give interviews!'

'Very true, but I've had a rethink.'

John stared at him in disbelief. The Italian multi-millionaire had always fiercely guarded his privacy, and since his divorce two years ago his attitude towards the press had toughened even further.

And yet here he was, inviting in the one journalist who in his opinion was trouble with a capital T. She always seemed to be nosing around at the moment; everywhere he went

Ms Keyes was there, asking questions about their takeover of the Sienna confectionery company. A deal that was supposed to be secret and was in the last sensitive stages of negotiation. It was a perfectly legitimate deal, but the woman somehow made him feel they were doing something wrong.

'So…why…?' John asked finally, as his thoughts crystallised and he remembered that this was Marco Lombardi he was talking to—a man renowned for being astute.

'There's an old saying, John, about keeping your friends close and your enemies closer. Let's just say I'm putting it into practice.'

John glanced back towards the monitor again. But he didn't really understand. He noticed Isobel Keyes was glancing impatiently at her watch. 'So what time is her appointment? Do you want me to take this paperwork away and work on it in the other office?'

'No.' Marco returned to the figures in front of him. 'Ms Keyes can wait; she's very lucky to have been invited here in the first place. So we will start as we mean to go on.'

'Ah!' Suddenly John understood. 'You're giving her the runaround until the deal is signed.'

'Not exactly. Keeping her occupied might be the more correct terminology.' Marco smiled. 'Now, let's concentrate on what's important, shall we?'

As John opened the top file he couldn't help but feel a dart of sympathy for the young woman waiting outside in her prim business suit. Right now she was probably feeling pretty pleased with herself for gaining an interview with the elusive multi-millionaire. But she didn't stand a chance in hell if she was thinking of pitting her wits against Marco Lombardi.

Isobel was not in any way pleased about this situation. An hour ago she'd been on the verge of finding out exactly what was going on within the Sienna company. She'd been granted an interview with one of the Sienna shareholders, and then at the last minute the interview had been cancelled and out of the blue her editor had ordered her to drop the story.

'I've got something better for you,' Claudia had gushed with excitement. 'I've just had a phone call from our editorial director. Can you believe it? Marco Lombardi has agreed to give the *Daily Banner* an exclusive interview!'

Isobel had indeed been stunned. She'd tried to get an interview with Marco on a few occasions and had never got past his secretary. 'Is he going to talk to me about his plans for taking over the Sienna confectionery company?' she'd asked hopefully.

'Isobel, forget about pursuing the business side of the story. What we want is a personal insight into Marco's life, and the real facts behind his divorce. That's the story readers really want, and it will be like gold dust for the paper.'

The word smokescreen came to mind.

Isobel clenched and unclenched her hands. She knew most journalists would have been ecstatic to get an interview with the handsome Italian. But she was a serious reporter, not a tattler of gossip. She didn't want to do an in-depth interview about Marco's love-life! She wanted to write a real story about people's jobs being on the line.

As far as she was concerned her paper had struck a deal with the devil—but, as usual, commercial considerations ruled the day, she reminded herself angrily.

'You can go up now, Ms Keyes.' The receptionist smiled over at her. 'Mr Lombardi's office is on the top floor.'

Hallelujah, Isobel thought sardonically as she glanced at her watch. He'd only been keeping her waiting for over an hour. And of course he had done that on purpose too.

As the lift swept her upwards, Isobel tried to compose herself. She had no choice now but to swallow her principles and give the paper the article they wanted, but it really did infuriate her. Because Marco was the type of man she despised. The type of man who did exactly as he pleased, regardless of the consequences, regardless of who he might hurt. And she had reason to know that more than most—because this was the man who had bought out her grandfather's firm eleven years ago, and had then systematically torn it apart, breaking her grandfather's heart in the process.

As far as she was concerned, Marco was a ruthless charlatan. And frankly she couldn't understand why there was so much speculation over his divorce. The reason he'd split with his wife seemed blindingly obvious to Isobel—he'd always been a womaniser. So much so that people had been stunned when he had announced he was getting married. And since his divorce he'd been pictured in the press with a different woman every week. Some sections of the press had even dubbed him a heartbreaker, for heaven's sake!

As the lift doors swished open Isobel took a deep breath and reminded herself—as she always did when working on a story—that she couldn't allow preconceived ideas to cloud her judgement.

'This way, Ms Keyes.' A secretary stepped forward to open a door into an office with sweeping panoramic views out across London. But it wasn't the view that held Isobel's attention. It was the man seated behind the large desk

She had heard so much about him over the years that now, suddenly face to face with her nemesis, she felt slightly unnerved.

Marco was absorbed in some paperwork and didn't look up as she approached slowly. 'Ah, Ms Keyes, I presume.' He murmured the words absently, as if he were only half aware of her presence. His English pronunciation was perfect, but more disturbingly she noticed that his velvet Italian accent sizzled with sex appeal.

He was wearing a white shirt left casually open at the strong column of his neck. Isobel noticed how the colour contrasted with the olive tones of his skin and the dark silky thickness of his hair.

She stopped next to the desk, and at the same time he looked up and their eyes locked. Inexplicably, her heart seemed to do a very peculiar flip.

He was incredibly good-looking, she thought hazily. His bone structure was strong, giving him an aura of determination and power, but it was his eyes that held her spellbound: they were the most amazing eyes she had ever seen—dark, smouldering, and extraordinarily intense.

She didn't know why she was so taken aback by him—it wasn't as if she hadn't already known he was attractive. There were snatched photographs of the thirty-five-year-old in the press all the time. And women were always raving about how handsome he was. But Isobel had always maintained that she couldn't quite see what all the fuss was about—she didn't like the guy, and as far as she was concerned a lack of moral substance overshadowed mere good-looks any day. It was therefore a total shock to find herself so....mesmerised.

'Sit down and make yourself comfortable.' He waved her towards the chair opposite him, and she had to shake herself mentally.

What the hell was wrong with her? She was staring at him like an idiot! And meanwhile she was well aware that his eyes had moved over her with a look that could only at best be described as quizzically indifferent. No surprise there.

Isobel knew there was no way she could match up to the women Marco would be drawn to—for a start his ex-wife was a film star, rated as one of the world's most beautiful women. By comparison Isobel was nothing—just a Plain Jane. Her clothes were businesslike, her figure bordered on being too curvaceous, and her long dark hair—although shiny and well cut—was held back from her face in a manner that was purely practical.

But that was her style. She didn't want to be overtly feminine or glamorous. She wanted to get on with her work and to be treated seriously. And she certainly didn't want to attract men like Marco Lombardi, she reminded herself fiercely. Her father had been a womaniser, and she knew how someone like that could devastate lives.

The reminder helped to snap her back to reality.

'So, Mr Lombardi, it seems you have succeeded in diverting attention away from your proposed bid to buy Sienna,' she remarked crisply as she took the seat opposite.

Marco had been about to finish his paperwork and keep her waiting a little longer, but he found himself looking over at her again. 'Have I, indeed?' he countered wryly. Her cool, businesslike tones surprised him. Most women flirted with him. Even when they were being businesslike they softened their questions with a fluttering of eyelashes and a surfeit of smiles. Isobel Keyes, it seemed, wasn't going to conform on either front.

'You know very well that you have,' she retaliated. 'And we both know it's the only reason I've been granted this interview.'

Interesting, he thought as he gave her demure appearance another quick glance.

His first assessment of her, when he'd seen her on the security monitors, had been that she was a staid little mouse—someone who would probably be easily fobbed off with an interview. Now he was busy reassessing her.

'You seem very certain about your facts.'

'I am certain.' She angled her chin up a little. 'I saw your accountant at the Sienna offices this morning.'

'You probably did. He's a free agent—he can go where he wants.'

'He goes where you send him,' she countered quickly.

He hadn't noticed her eyes until now. The feisty sparkle in them made them glow a deep emerald-green.

His gaze swept slowly over her face again. He'd originally thought that she was in her late twenties—probably because he hadn't looked at her that closely. But now he realised that it was just the way she was dressed that made her seem older, and that she was possibly nearer to twenty-one. Nice skin too. She might have been passably attractive if she made more of an effort with herself. The hairstyle did nothing for her, and she was wearing little or no make-up. As for the clothes… His eyes swept downwards. They were verging on boring.

No Italian woman would be caught dead in a blouse like that…especially with it buttoned right up to the neck! Her waist was small, and she appeared well endowed. That blouse would definitely benefit from being unbuttoned a few notches, he thought distractedly.

Isobel suddenly noticed his sweeping assessment of her appearance, and as his dark eyes moved boldly back to her face she found herself heating up inside with consternation. Why was he looking at her like that? It was almost as if he were weighing up her desirability.

The thought made her heat up even more.

Hell, she was blushing! How embarrassing was that, when she disliked Marco so intensely? She wouldn't be interested in him if he was the last man left in the universe, and she knew damn well that Marco would never be interested in her!

Maybe he looked at every woman like that—or maybe he was trying to distract her from their conversation. Now, that was a possibility.

'So, are you trying to tell me that you have no interest in buying Sienna Confectionery?' She sat up a little straighter in her chair.

Marco smiled slowly. He had to admire her tenacity, but it was time he reined her in. 'I take it you want to make this a business interview?' he murmured smoothly.

'No!' Her skin flared with even more heat as she imagined the hullabaloo at the paper if she ignored the brief they'd given her. 'I was just saying that…I know what is going on.'

His lips curved in an almost derogatory smile. Then he

reached for the phone on his desk. 'Deirdre, arrange for my limousine to pick me up outside in ten minutes.'

Isobel could feel her heart thudding nervously against her chest. 'Are you going to bail out on me because I dared question you on a subject you don't want to discuss?' She forced herself to hold his gaze, but inside she was suddenly terrified. Hell, if she mucked up with this interview she could find herself out of a job! The paper was desperate for an exclusive—in fact every paper in the land was desperate for an interview with Marco. Her kudos as a reporter would be out of the window if she messed this up.

Marco didn't answer her straight away, and her nerves stretched as she thought about the hefty mortgage she had taken on when she had moved apartments last year. She needed this job.

'Look, Mr Lombardi, I'll be honest with you. I'd rather do a business interview—because that's what I do. I'm a business correspondent. But the *Daily Banner*, in its wisdom, has sent me here because you've done a deal with them. You said you'd give the paper an exclusive glimpse into your life. So how about it? Because if I don't get this story… Well…'

'You're in trouble.' He finished her sentence for her and smiled. 'Why, Ms Keyes, are you throwing yourself on my mercy?'

He knew damn well that she was in a predicament—because *he'd* placed her in it, she thought furiously. With difficulty, she tried to remain calm. 'Yes, I suppose I am.'

He noticed how the husky admission almost stuck in her throat, and one dark eyebrow lifted mockingly.

'Did you bring your passport?'

'My passport?' The question caught her off guard, and she stared at him in apprehension. 'Why would I need that?'

'I offered your paper an exclusive glimpse into my life, Ms Keyes—and I travel quite extensively.' As he was talking to her Marco was packing away his papers into a briefcase. 'I have meetings in Italy and in Nice tomorrow, and I'm leaving in just under an hour. So if you want your story you're going to have to tag along with me.'

'Nobody told me that! I was told you were inviting me into your home—'

'I am. My home is in the South of France.'

'But you have a place here—in Kensington!' Her voice rose slightly. 'Don't you?'

Marco closed his case and looked over at her. 'I also have houses in Paris, Rome and Barbados, but I'm based on the Riviera.'

'I see.' She swallowed hard on a tight knot of panic. 'Well, unfortunately I haven't packed for a trip to France, and I have no passport with me.'

Marco almost felt sorry for her—almost, but not quite. Because she was a journalist, and as far as he was concerned journalists were the piranhas of this world, feeding off other people's lives. 'Seems like you are in a bit of a bind, then, doesn't it? Your editor will be disappointed.' He noticed impassively that she seemed to lose all colour from her face at that.

'Look, if you could drive to the airport via my apartment it would take me fifteen—maybe twenty minutes tops to throw my stuff together,' she suggested in desperation.

'I don't have twenty minutes to spare,' Marco told her tersely as he rose to his feet and reached for the jacket of his suit. 'But in the interests of goodwill I'll give you five.'

As Isobel looked up at him she saw the gleam of amusement in the darkness of his eyes, and she realised that he'd never had any intention of leaving her behind. He was playing with her as a cat would play with a mouse before pouncing for the kill.

She suddenly wanted to run a million miles from him—because this didn't bode well for her interview.

'When you're ready,' he grated impatiently as she made no move to stand up.

Hurriedly she got to her feet. What else could she do but go along with this?

CHAPTER TWO

As ISOBEL followed Marco out of the Lombardi offices, a group of waiting paparazzi across the road sprang into life. There were insistent shouts for them to look over towards the cameras, and calls for Marco to answer questions. They wanted to know where he was going, who Isobel was, if he had spoken to his ex-wife recently.

Marco seemed unfazed by the situation and made no comment, but the intrusion took Isobel by surprise. She wasn't used to being on this side of press attention, and the flash photography and the unrelenting questions felt aggressive. She was almost glad to reach the seclusion of Marco's limousine, with its smoked glass windows.

'Friends of yours?' Marco asked sardonically as he climbed in behind her and took a seat opposite.

'No, of course not!' The question startled her. 'I have absolutely nothing to do with them! They're like a pack of hyenas.'

'Your point being…?'

She was starting to get used to that derisive dry edge to his voice. 'My point being that is not *my* style of journalism.'

'Ah, yes, I forgot—you are a serious reporter, only interested in business.'

She raised her chin slightly. 'And I'm good at my job—well, I must be, mustn't I? It's the only reason you've agreed to give my paper an exclusive.'

'I hate to burst your bubble,' he drawled, 'but the main reason I've decided to give the press an exclusive is because of incidents like the one you have just witnessed, where I'm constantly pestered by reporters who want to know everything about me down to what I've had for my breakfast.'

Isobel had to agree that the situation had been unpleasant. She glanced out of the window and noticed that even though the chauffeur had pulled the limousine out into traffic the paparazzi were following on motorbikes.

'And then there are the important business deals that have been wholly jeopardised by unwarranted press attention and ill-timed sensationalistic reporting,' Marco continued sardonically. 'Ring any bells?'

She frowned. 'I hope you're not suggesting—'

'I'm not suggesting anything.' He cut across her firmly. 'I'm telling you why I've taken the decision to give a one-off in-depth interview—I'm hoping it's going to be an interview to end all interviews. And that I shall get some peace and quiet after it.'

'And you just happened to offer this opportunity to the *Daily Banner*?' she asked archly.

'I did my homework. And surprisingly your name has cropped up quite a few times over the last say…eighteen months. There was your report about my deal with the Alexia retail group…a few less than flattering columns about my takeover of a supermarket chain, and a very scathing article about my—I quote—"domination of the Rolands Group". Shall I go on?'

'No, you have no need to go on, I get the picture,' Isobel muttered hastily. OK, she *had* singled his business out for some in-depth coverage last year, but only because he had done a lot of buying and selling, and she had always done her research. 'I never said you had done anything wrong or illegal. Nothing I've written has been untrue.'

'But it has verged on scaremongering.'

'I'm a business correspondent. It's my job to report to the public about what is going on.'

He nodded. 'And now it is your job to follow me around and report on that.'

She stared at him. 'Like a kind of punishment?' The words fell from her lips before she could stop them.

Marco stared at her, and then he laughed. 'I feel I should remind you at this point that every journalist in the land would probably love to change places with you right now.'

His arrogance was extremely infuriating—and so was the fact that he was probably right. 'Yes, I do realise that.' She glared at him. 'And I'm not complaining. I'm just saying—'

'That you are a serious journalist who would rather write about my business ventures than my dietary requirements?' he finished for her, his eyes glinting with amusement.

'Yes, exactly. I mean, let's face it, the world hardly needs another celeb interview, does it?' She spoke impulsively. and then hastily tried to correct the mistake. 'That doesn't mean I don't *want* to interview you—because of course I do!'

'Relax—I know exactly what you mean. And I'm more than happy to talk about my businesses and my rise to the top of the financial markets. In fact, that is what I would like to focus on.'

Isobel was sure any business information he gave her would be very one-sided, and she wanted to say, *Yeah, right* in a very derogatory tone, but she didn't dare.

'Well, I wouldn't worry about it,' she said instead. 'Because it turns out that most people are only interested in your love-life.'

'Is that so?' His dark eyes held with hers.

'Yes… Bizarre, but there it is.'

Marco smiled. He was starting to like Ms Isobel Keyes. Had he hit the jackpot and engaged the one journalist who wasn't interested in digging the dirt on his marriage?

'So what exactly *is* the story with your divorce?' she

asked suddenly, her green eyes narrowing. 'Because every-one thought that you and Lucinda did seem like the perfect couple.'

No—he hadn't hit the jackpot, he berated himself. Like every other journalist she was a breed apart—a sub-species for whom no subject was too personal to have a good dig around in.

'Let's not get ahead of ourselves, Ms Keyes,' he said coolly.

Was it her imagination, or was his expression suddenly shuttered? Certainly the gleam of amusement in his voice had disappeared. Strange… She had expected that reaction when she talked about his business dealings, not his relationships.

Maybe he just didn't like the fact that the press knew he was a womaniser? Maybe that was another reason he had agreed to this interview—to try and reinvent himself?

Well, if he thought she was going to fall for that he had a shock coming, she thought fiercely.

The limousine was slowing down. And as she looked out she realised they were pulling up outside her flat.

'OK, I won't be long,' she murmured as the chauffeur got out and opened the passenger door for her.

One of her neighbours was walking past, and the woman almost fell over in surprise when she saw Isobel getting out of a limousine, closely followed by Marco Lombardi.

'Don't you think it might be better if you waited in the lim-ousine?' Isobel said nervously as he walked with her towards the front door.

'No, I don't. What's the matter? Are you frightened there might be gossip about us?'

'Of course not!' She slanted a look up at him and noticed that the amusement was back in the darkness of his gaze. Yes, he probably thought that was oh-so-funny. As if anyone would seriously think that he would be interested in her when he had his pick of the world's most glamorous women.

The paparazzi had roared into the road now, and the usually quiet cul-de-sac was suddenly chaotic as once again they started to take photographs, shouting for Marco to look over.

Isobel was so flustered that she could hardly get her key in the lock fast enough, and calmly Marco reached to take it from her. The touch of his hand against hers was a shock to the system, and she jerked away from him abruptly.

'There you go.' He pushed the door open for her and looked over at her with a raised eyebrow. 'Are the press rattling you?'

'No, of course not.' The truth of the matter was that the paparazzi weren't bothering her half as much as he was.

'After you, then.'

'Thanks.' What on earth was wrong with her? Isobel wondered angrily as she stepped past him into the hallway. It was as if her senses were all on heightened alert around him.

And she had never felt more nervous in all her life as he followed her up the stairs to her first-floor flat.

She supposed it was just the strangeness of the situation. She'd disliked this man for so long from a distance, and now here he was stepping into her sitting room, acting as if he had every right to be here. In fact, his presence seemed to dominate the small flat.

Isobel watched as his gaze moved slowly over his surroundings, and for some reason she found herself looking at the place through his eyes.

The rooms weren't what you would call spacious, and her second-hand furniture looked shabby in the cold grey light of the afternoon. She was willing to bet that Marco's designer Italian suit had cost more money than all her possessions lumped together.

The thought brought her back to reality. OK, she didn't have a lot of money, but that was no reason to feel embarrassed or ashamed. She'd had no helping hand in life—she'd come from a poverty-stricken background and worked hard to get to where she was now. What was more, she had always treated people fairly along the way—which was more than Marco could say.

He'd practically bankrupted her grandfather's business, until the old man had been forced to sell out to him because he just couldn't afford to compete with him. And then as soon as Marco had taken over the firm he'd lost no time in restructuring—which had basically meant firing most of the staff. Isobel's father had been amongst the people in the first wave of redundancies.

She could still remember the shock in her father's eyes when he'd come home to tell them. She remembered how he'd sat at the kitchen table and buried his head in his hands. He'd kept saying that there had been no need to make people redundant—that the company was very profitable. And her grandfather had said the same.

'It's greed, Isobel,' he had said. 'Some people aren't content with making a healthy profit. They're only happy when they are making an obscene profit.'

Isobel remembered those words as she looked over at Marco. He'd been a couple of years older than she was now— about twenty-four—when he'd bought her grandfather's firm and sacked half the workforce. And then he'd gone on to sell the business twelve months later for a *very* obscene profit, as far as Isobel was concerned.

And it seemed Marco had repeated this move in other businesses time and time again, making him a multi-millionaire before the age of thirty.

She wondered if he ever had pangs of conscience about the way he made his money.

As soon as the thought crossed her mind she dismissed it as absurd. Marco wasn't the type to think deeply about other people's feelings. As demonstrated by the way he'd walked out on his wife after just eighteen months of marriage, and the way he changed the women in his life faster than some people changed the sheets on the bed.

Something he had in common with her father, as it turned out.

She turned away from him. 'I'll just throw a few things in a bag, I won't be long.'

'See that you're not,' he said laconically. 'I meant it when I said you'd got five minutes.'

Hurriedly she moved through to her bedroom and opened the wardrobe. What on earth should she pack for a night in the South of France? she wondered. She didn't have a lot of summer gear, but then it probably wouldn't be that hot as it was only May.

She glanced around as there was a knock on the door and it opened behind her. 'Four minutes and counting,' Marco told her as he leaned against the doorframe.

'For heaven's sake, I'm going as fast as I can.' She flung a pair of jeans and a T-shirt into an overnight case, and then moved to rifle through her nightwear and her underwear drawer. 'Do you think you could give me a moment's privacy?' she asked through gritted teeth as she looked around at him.

'Don't mind me.' He smiled, but instead of moving out of her room he came further in, and walked over towards the window to look out.

At least he had his back to her, but the guy had an unmitigated gall, she thought furiously. She selected a nightshirt and some underwear and threw it in the case.

'Don't forget your passport,' he reminded her nonchalantly. 'That's all that really matters.'

'Of course I won't.'

'Good.' He adjusted the blinds a little, so that he could look down to the road. And she realised that he had only come in here because it was the one room with a clear view out over the front of the property.

'Are the paparazzi still there?' she asked curiously.

'Unfortunately, yes.' He snapped the blinds closed and turned to look at her again. 'So you'd better get a move on—because otherwise you could be splashed all over the front page tomorrow and dubbed my new lover,' he added lazily.

He watched with amusement as her cheeks flushed bright red.

'I very much doubt that, Mr Lombardi,' she told him stiffly, wondering if this was his feeble attempt at trying to dissociate himself from the many women he'd been pictured with since his divorce.

'Do you? Why is that?'

'Because…' *What kind of question was that to ask her?* she wondered in annoyance. 'Well…because I am very obviously not your type.'

'Aren't you?' He looked across at her teasingly.

'No, I'm not!' She was starting to think he enjoyed winding her up. 'Everyone knows that you go for very glamorous blondes,' she added snappily, and tried to return her attention to her suitcase. But she was finding it really hard to concentrate on packing now; she was far too distracted by the way he was watching her. 'And just for the record you're not my type either,' she added for good measure as she glanced up at him.

He didn't look in the least bit bothered. In fact one dark eyebrow was raised mockingly, as if he didn't believe that for one moment. The guy was far too sure of himself, she thought heatedly. Probably because no woman had ever said no to him.

'And do you think that it matters for one moment that you are not my usual type?' he asked.

'Matters—in what way?' She was confused for a moment.

'Well, the press sensationalise everything. You could be my

maiden aunt and they would still think there was something going on between us.'

'That is not true!'

His dark eyes gleamed. 'Spoken like a loyal member of the press.'

'Well, maybe I am.' She shrugged. 'But I know we are not that easily bamboozled.'

'Bamboozled enough to think I only go for blondes,' he said with a smile. 'When in actual fact I have a penchant for the odd brunette.'

She felt her body burn as his dark gaze swept slowly over her. She knew he was only joking, but she found the intensity of his gaze wholly unnerving,

He was a total wind-up merchant, she thought uncomfortably as she turned away. There was no way on God's earth that he would ever be interested in her—nor her in him, she reminded herself fiercely. She knew it—he knew it—and pretending anything else even for a bit of fun was just hideously embarrassing. They were at different ends of a very wide spectrum.

She closed her case with a thud. 'I'll just go and get my toiletries, and then I'm ready.'

Marco watched as she hurried away from him. He didn't think he had ever met a woman so determined not to flirt with him, he thought with a smile. The strange thing was that the more she backed away from him the more intrigued he became.

He glanced idly around at her possessions. From what he could judge she seemed to live here alone. The place was almost minimalist in design, plainly furnished and yet striking. A bit like its owner, he thought with amusement. His gaze moved over to her workstation in the corner. The desk was tidy, but a huge stack of paper and notebooks led him to believe she probably did a lot of work from home. There were a few reference books—huge, serious tomes on economics. Was that her bedtime reading? he wondered with a grin.

There were also a couple of photographs in frames, and he glanced at them. One was of a woman in her fifties and the other was of an older guy of about seventy. Were they her parents? Her father looked much older than her mother. Marco looked more closely. Actually, the guy looked familiar.

Isobel came back into the room, and Marco turned his attention to more important things. He had a lot of paperwork to do, and a flight to catch. 'Time is marching on,' he reminded her, glancing at his watch.

'Yes, I do realise that—and I'm ready when you are.' She put the cosmetics bag into her case and zipped it up.

'Really? Well, I'm impressed,' he said with a smile. 'You have half a minute to spare and…' his gaze moved to the case in her hand '…probably the smallest amount of luggage of any woman I've ever taken away for the weekend.'

Did he have to make everything sound so damn intimate? she wondered uncomfortably. 'Well, that's because you're not taking me away for the *weekend*.'

'I think you'll find that I am,' he countered with a smile.

'We are going away on a business trip for one night,' she maintained firmly. 'And as today is only Thursday, that hardly qualifies even marginally as going away for the weekend.'

She really was an enigma, Marco thought with amusement. Most women fell over themselves to spend time with him, and yet she seemed almost horrorstruck by the thought.

'You can make your own way home tomorrow, if you wish,' he said easily. 'But I doubt your in-depth interview will be complete.'

As she looked over at him her eyes seemed to be impossibly wide and too large for her face. 'Well, we shall just have to try and move things along faster,' she said with determination.

'You can try.' He grinned. 'But I have a lot of business to attend to over the next forty-eight hours, so you will have to fit in around me. I think it would probably be more realistic to say that you will be in France until at least Monday.'

'You've got to be joking!'

'Not at all.'

Their eyes seemed to clash across the small dividing space between them.

She didn't want to spend a few days with him. The very thought of it made her blood pressure go into hyper-drive.

'I really don't think I will be able to stay that long,' she murmured uncomfortably.

'Well, as I said, it's up to you.' He shrugged.

But it wasn't up to her, was it? she thought nervously. And he knew that—knew that she would be forced to hang around until she got the story that her paper expected. A story that would be superficial at best.

And meanwhile he would finalise his deal for Sienna and start to take the company apart at the seams. Because that was what he did.

Isobel glanced away from him.

She hated that he could get away with it. Hated the fact that he was cocooned by his wealth—the type who seemed to glide though life unaffected by other people's problems.

But she didn't have to let him get away with it, she thought suddenly. Just because she could no longer write about his business dealings in depth, it didn't mean she couldn't expose him in her article for the uncaring, arrogant womaniser that he was.

Feeling a little bit better at the thought, she reached for her suitcase.

Marco thought that he was being oh-so-clever, but she would have the last laugh, she told herself firmly.

CHAPTER THREE

USUALLY when Isobel travelled through airports she had to wait in queues to check in, and then there would be more queues to get through Security and onto the plane. Travelling with Marco, however, was a whole new experience. There was to be no mundane waiting around for Marco. He breezed through everything at VIP level, and people couldn't do enough for him. It was *Yes, Mr Lombardi—No, Mr Lombardi—Nothing is too much trouble, Mr Lombardi.*

Isobel was absolutely amazed by the speed of the whole process—from check-in to getting aboard the aircraft. And then when they did step on board she was even more astounded to find it was his company jet and that they were the only passengers.

Just another little glimpse into the excesses of Marco Lombardi's world, she thought as she looked around.

They were soon travelling at thirty thousand feet, seated opposite each other in comfortable black leather seats that were larger than her sofa at home. Marco had swivelled his chair slightly, so that he could take advantage of the conference facilities aboard, and since take-off he'd been in a meeting with his corporate strategist in Rome, to discuss a project they were working on in Italy.

Isobel would have loved to know more details, but unfortunately that was all Marco had told her, and she couldn't understand anything he was saying because he was speaking in Italian. For a while she'd tried to pass the time by reading one of the newspapers the cabin crew had handed out to them earlier, but she'd found it hard to concentrate because she had been drawn to listening to Marco as he talked, mesmerised by the attractive, deep tones.

There was something deeply passionate about the Italian language. Marco sounded fiercely intent one moment and almost lyrically provocative the next. So much so that she found herself not only listening, but also covertly watching him. The accent combined with his good looks was a power-fully compelling combination…hard to pull away from.

No man had a right to be so sexually attractive, she thought distractedly. Especially a man who was so completely ruthless. But…hell, he really was gorgeous.

He glanced over at that moment and caught her watching him, and as their eyes met she felt a surge of heat so intense it made her feel dizzy.

How pathetic was that? she thought angrily, looking swiftly away. She should be focusing her mind on structuring the article she wanted to write about him, on revealing the true Marco Lombardi—not on idly admiring his looks!

Being handsome didn't mean a thing. Her father had been a good-looking man, suave, sophisticated, a definite hit with women. Even as a young child Isobel had noticed the way women smiled at him. She had been fiercely proud of her handsome dad—had hero-worshiped him.

And she had been naively unaware that the only reason he'd stayed around was the lure of her grandfather's money.

When his father-in-law had sold the business and he had been made redundant Martin Keyes had been self-pitying at first. But two months down the line, when her grandfather had died and it had been revealed that all his fortune had gone on death duties and taxes, he had been furious. Isobel had heard the arguments raging into the night. Had heard his parting shots to her mother—that the lure of the family business had been all that had kept him in the marriage, and that he felt as if he had wasted twelve years of his life. Then she had heard the slam of the door.

When she'd gone downstairs her mother had been sitting on the floor, sobbing. 'He said he never loved us, Isobel,' she had cried.

She could still remember that moment vividly—her mother's heart-rending sobs, the shock and the feeling of fear and helplessness, and also the knowledge that she had to be strong for her mum's sake.

Life had been tough after that. Her mother had struggled to cope, both financially and emotionally, and for the first year Isobel had found it hard to believe that her dad had truly abandoned them completely. She'd dreamed he would come back, that he hadn't meant those cruel words. Her birthday and Christmas had come and gone without any contact. Then one day quite suddenly, without warning, she'd seen him again outside her school gates. She'd thought he was waiting for her and her heart had leapt. But he hadn't been waiting for her. He'd been with another woman, and as Isobel had watched from a distance she'd seen a child from one of the junior classes running towards them. As Isobel had slowly approached they'd all got into a Mercedes parked at the kerb and driven away.

The really awful thing was that her father had seen her— but he hadn't even acknowledged her with so much as a smile. It was as if she had ceased to exist and was just a stranger.

She'd grown up that day. There had been no more day-dreams of a happy-ever-after. And she supposed it had made her into the person she was today—independent and a realist. Certainly not the type to be drawn to a man just because of his looks.

Marco had finished his conversation and was packing some of his papers away.

'We have about twenty minutes before we land,' he said to her suddenly. 'Would you like a drink?'

Even before she answered him he was summoning one of the cabin crew.

'I'll have a whisky, please, Michelle,' he said easily as a member of staff appeared instantly beside him. Then he looked over at Isobel enquiringly.

'Just an orange juice, please.'

Marco turned his chair around to face her and she felt as if she was in a sophisticated bar somewhere—not on an aircraft heading out to the Mediterranean.

'We seem to be ahead of schedule,' Marco said as he looked at his watch. 'Which means we will be arriving before it gets dark. That's good. It will give you a chance to catch a little of the spectacular scenery along the coastline.'

'That would be nice. I can add a description of arriving at your house to my article. Do you live far from Nice Airport?'

'My residence is nearer to the Italian border—about half an hour's drive away. But we will be flying into my private airstrip just ten minutes away from the house.'

'You have your own airstrip?'

'Yes. Sometimes the roads are very busy getting in and out of Nice, so it frees up a little time—makes life easier.' He shrugged in that Latin way of his.

'You are a man in a hurry,' she reflected wryly, and he laughed.

'It's certainly true that there are never enough hours in the day.'

He had a very attractive laugh, and his eyes were warm as they fell on her—so warm, in fact, that for a moment she found herself forgetting what she wanted to say next.

The stewardess brought their drinks. Isobel noticed how she smiled at Marco when he thanked her.

He probably had that affect on every woman he looked at, she thought.

She was about to pour some orange juice into her glass,

but he did it for her. 'I take it you don't drink?' he asked conversationally as he passed her glass over to her.

'Thanks. I do, but not when I'm working.' She forced herself to sound businesslike. OK, jetting into the South of France with this man was probably every woman's dream, but she had to stay focused. Marco Lombardi wasn't the type of man to relax with. He was too smooth…too practised at getting exactly what he wanted. And what he wanted from her was probably to lull her into a false sense of alliance so that she would write about how wonderful he was. Well, that wasn't going to happen. She wasn't that easily fooled.

She just wished he wouldn't look at her with such close attention. She sat up rigidly in her seat, ramrod-straight, and tried to cultivate a definite no-nonsense look in her eyes. 'So, do you travel around the world a lot in your private jet?'

'You sound like you are going to shine a light in my eyes and cross-examine me on my carbon footprint,' he murmured in amusement.

'Do I…? Well, that wasn't my intention.' She shifted a little uncomfortably in her chair. 'I'm just trying to gather a few facts about you for my readers, that's all.'

'Hmm…' He lounged back and looked at her for a long moment, and she could feel her heart suddenly starting to speed up.

'Tell me, do you ever relax?' he asked.

The suddenly personal question took her aback. 'Yes, of course I do, Mr Lombardi. But as I said, not—'

'When you are working.' He finished the sentence for her, a gleam of amusement in his expression. 'OK, that's fine. But I've got a suggestion to make. I think, as we are about to spend a few days and nights together at my home, that we should drop the formalities—don't you?'

The words combined with that sexy Italian accent made alarm bells start to ring inside her. Did he have to make the

situation sound quite so…intimate? she wondered apprehensively.

'So you can call me Marco,' he continued without waiting
for a reply, 'and I'll call you Izzy. '

'Actually, nobody calls me Izzy,' she interrupted.

'Good. I like to be different.'

He smiled as he noticed the fire in her eyes, the flare of
heightened colour in her cheeks. It was strange, but he found
himself enjoying rattling that cool edge of reserve that she
seemed determined to hide behind. 'We'll be starting our
descent into the sunny Côte d'Azur in a few minutes, and it
is not the continental way to be so uptight,' he added.

'I'm not uptight, Mr Lombardi—'

'Marco,' he corrected her softly. 'Go on you can say it…
Marco…' He enunciated the name playfully, his Italian accent
rolling attractively over it.

'OK…Marco.' She shrugged, and then for good measure
added, 'Now you try *ISOBEL*…' She rolled her tongue over
her name with the same emphasis, and then slanted him a
defiant look that made him laugh.

'You see? You are getting into the continental spirit of
things already,' he teased.

Their eyes held for a moment, then he smiled at her.

It was the oddest thing, but she suddenly felt a most disturbing jolt in the pit of her stomach—as if she had stepped
off a cliff and was plummeting fast to the ground.

'Anyway, I…I think we are getting a bit off track,' she
murmured, trying desperately to gather her senses again.

'Are we?'

'Yes, it's best…you know…to keep things strictly businesslike.'

There was a defensive, almost fierce glitter in her eyes
now as she looked at him, but there was also an underlying
glimmer of vulnerability. It was almost as if she was scared
of lowering her guard around him, he thought suddenly.

The notion intrigued him, and for a moment his gaze moved over the creamy perfection of her skin, the cupid's bow of her mouth, then lower to the full soft curves of her figure hidden beneath that buttoned up blouse.

Their eyes met again, and she looked even more self-conscious.

Was it an act or not? There was something very alluring about that mix of wide-eyed innocence and hostile attitude. As if she could give as good as she could get—a wary kitten that might purr most agreeably if handled correctly.

As soon as the thought crossed his mind it irritated him! She was a member of the press—and there was nothing vulnerable about a journalist who was hungry for a story, he reminded himself firmly.

'Don't worry, Izzy, I won't allow us to get too far off track,' he grated mockingly.

The pilot's voice interrupted them, to say they were starting their final descent and would be touching down in precisely fifteen minutes.

Isobel watched as Marco reached to pick up the rest of the papers he'd been working on earlier.

When his eyes had slipped down over her body she'd felt so hot inside that she could hardly breathe. And she felt foolish now…foolish for imagining for one moment that he was flirting with her.

In reality he was probably laughing at her. The little plain mouse who melted when he smiled at her.

The thought made her burn with embarrassment—because she *had* melted.

Acknowledging that fact even for a moment made her feel very ill at ease, and angrily she tried to dismiss it.

She was here to get a story, and she was totally focused.

As Marco put his work away into his briefcase the plane hit an air pocket, and a few sheets from a report slid across the polished surface of the table and fell onto the floor at her feet.

She bent to pick them up for him, and couldn't resist glancing at the pages as she did. Unfortunately they were all in Italian, but she managed to catch the printed heading: '*Porzione*'.

She looked over at Marco as she handed it back to him. 'What is that?'

'Nothing that needs to concern you,' he said, tucking it safely away into his briefcase.

Which almost certainly meant it *would* concern her, she thought sardonically. It was probably some poor unfortunate company that he was about to gobble up and spit out.

'Don't forget to fasten your safety belt,' he said as he settled back into his seat.

'No, I won't. Thanks.' She buckled up, and then glanced away from him out of the window.

Sitting opposite him like this was completely unnerving; there was just something about him that put all of her sensory nerve-endings on high alert.

Porzione—she tried to focus on practicalities, telling herself that she should remember the name and look it up on the internet later. OK, she wasn't supposed to write about his business dealings, but that didn't stop her doing a little research and maybe adding a line here and there about his ruthless takeover deals.

She tried to focus on that, and on the bright blue of the sky, on the sound of the engines as the powerful jet geared up for landing—on anything except that moment of attraction she had felt for Marco a little while ago.

It was her imagination, she told herself fiercely. She would never fall under the spell of a man who was a known heart-breaker. And she didn't buy all that stuff that people spouted about desire overruling common sense. Maybe that happened to other people, but it wasn't going to happen to her. She was far too practical for that; she always weighed everything up logically. Probably because she'd seen from her own childhood just what could happen if you fell for the wrong man.

Isobel's mother had never really recovered from her divorce. She'd suffered from depression for a long time afterwards, with Isobel taking on the role of carer at some points. Once in a weak moment she'd even confessed to Isobel that she was still in love with her ex-husband.

How could you love someone who had treated you so badly? That confession had shocked Isobel beyond words. And she had always vowed that *she* would never allow a man to get her into that state, and that she would always be in control of her emotions.

She had pretty much kept to that vow. As a student at university she'd had a few boyfriends, but she'd always kept them at a distance—never allowing anyone to get too close and never getting into the whole casual sex scene. Instead she had thrown herself into her work. Coming from a single parent family, money had been tight. She'd had just one shot at getting her degree, and she'd been determined not to mess it up by getting sidetracked by a man.

After graduating she'd met Rob, and even though she'd liked him straight away she'd still kept her heart in reserve. Building her career had seemed more important. The thing about Rob was that he had seemed so safe and uncomplicated. He'd stayed around in the background, and little by little he had worked his way into her life. He'd gently told her that he didn't mind waiting until she was ready to make love, and that he respected her and admired her. He had even said that he held the same moral codes as her. That he knew all about heartbreak as his mother had walked out on him when he was young.

She'd felt sympathy for him when he told her that. And she'd started to trust him. Looking back, she supposed he'd become almost like a best friend. When he'd kissed her there had been no explosions of passion, but he'd made her laugh and he'd made her feel safe. And when he'd proposed to her it had seemed like the most natural thing in the world to say yes.

But Rob hadn't been the safe, reliable guy she had believed him to be. All those things he'd told her about fidelity being important had been lies. And when she'd caught him in his lies he had turned nasty—had told her that she'd driven him to it, that she was frigid.

Just thinking about it now brought a fresh dart of pain. It only went to show that no matter how careful you were there were no guarantees against heartache.

She closed her eyes for a few moments. At least she had found out her mistake before she had married him.

They were slowly starting to lose altitude, and the plane was juddering as currents of air hit it.

She'd been right all along: the best thing was to concentrate on a career, on being independent.

She opened her eyes and to her consternation found herself looking directly into Marco's dark, steady gaze. Immediately she felt the tug of some unfamiliar emotion twisting and turning deep inside her.

What was that? she wondered angrily. Because it wasn't desire. *Even if he did have the sexiest eyes of any man she had ever met.*

Hastily she looked away from him. Thoughts like that did not help this situation, she told herself angrily.

They were going through light, swirling clouds now. Then suddenly she could see the vivid sparkle of the Mediterranean beneath her, and ahead the shadowy outlines of the coast.

There were mountains rising sharply, and large swathes of forest.

Lower and lower they came, the engines whining softly, until Isobel thought that they might land in the sea. But just as she was starting to panic they skimmed in over a white beach and she saw a runway ahead.

A few minutes later they had touched down smoothly. And with a roar of the brakes they taxied to a halt.

'We are a bit early, but there should be a car outside to pick us up in five minutes,' Marco said casually as he unfastened his seat belt and stood up.

Isobel also got to her feet, and then wished she hadn't as she suddenly found herself too close to him in the confined space.

As he reached for his briefcase she sidestepped him so that she could open the overhead compartment and get her bag.

'Wait—I'll do that for you,' he offered, glancing around.

'No need. I've got it.' Hurriedly she opened the compartment, but the next moment a case slid out smacking into her shoulder.

'Are you OK?' Marco caught it before it could do any further damage, and swung it to the floor.

'Yes…' She grimaced and put a hand to her shoulder. 'I think so.'

'Let me look at you.' To her consternation, Marco put a hand on her arm and turned her to face him.

'No, really—I'm fine!' It was the weirdest thing, but the touch of his hand against her other arm made it throb more violently than her shoulder.

'It's torn your blouse.' Marco said as he looked at her. 'And you're bleeding.'

She glanced down and saw that he was right; there was a small crimson stain on the pristine white of her linen blouse. 'It's OK—it's only a scratch. I'll be fine.'

'It seems to be a bit more than a scratch. Do you want me to look at it for you?'

The mere suggestion was enough to make her temperature shoot through the roof of the plane. 'I most certainly do not!'

Her prim refusal amused him somewhat. 'Izzy, the cut is just fractionally below your collarbone. You will only have to unfasten the top three buttons of your blouse—it's hardly a striptease.'

The words made her skin flare with heat. 'It's fine... Really... I...'

He completely ignored her. 'Michelle, will you bring the first aid kit, please?' he called over his shoulder to the woman who had served them their drinks. Immediately she disappeared down to the bottom of the plane to comply. 'Now, let's have a look.' He turned his attention firmly back to her.

'Marco, I said I was fine—' She froze as he reached for the top button on her blouse and started to undo it.

Her heart was beating so loudly now that she felt it was filling the whole aircraft.

'Marco, I can do it myself!'

'At least you don't have any difficulty saying my name any more.' His dark eyes locked with hers and his lips twisted into a lazily attractive smile. For a panic-stricken moment she thought he was going to move on to the next button, but thankfully he didn't. He dropped his hands. 'Go ahead, then... You unfasten the buttons.'

'I'll do it later.'

'It's two little buttons, Izzy... Are you scared of me?' His eyebrow rose mockingly.

'No! Why would I be scared of you?' Angrily she reached up to comply—she was damned if she was going to let him think she was scared of him!

He noticed that her hands were trembling. He'd never had this effect on a woman before. He frowned as he saw the shadows in her eyes as she looked up at him... What was she so scared of? he wondered curiously.

'There! Happy?' She glared at him.

'I wouldn't go that far.' He said the words derisively, and noticed how she blushed even more, but this time she looked more humiliated than shy. He frowned and wished for some reason that he hadn't said that.

OK, she was a bit of a Plain Jane, and nowhere in the league of the women he usually dated, but there was also something…interesting about her.

Curiously he reached out and lightly stroked his hand over her collarbone, pushing the blouse back further until he could see the wound.

She wasn't prepared for the touch of his fingers against her skin; it sent a dart of sensual pleasure racing through her unlike anything she had ever experienced before. Horrified by her reaction to him, she could only stare up at him in consternation.

In the stillness of the cabin it was almost as if time stood still.

Marco smiled as he saw the flare of desire deep in the depths of her green eyes. *Now* he knew why she looked so scared…she definitely wasn't as immune to him as she'd been pretending all afternoon. That amused him…and for some strange reason even pleased him.

He noticed how she moistened her lips nervously, could see her breathing quickening by the rise and fall of her chest.

He wondered how it would feel to kiss her…

As soon as the thought crossed his mind he dismissed it. She was a journalist, for heaven's sake…one of a breed he despised! They were hard-bitten, uncaring, trouble-stirring… He could go on for ever listing the reasons he hated the press.

His gaze moved away from her lips and back to the cut on her collarbone. 'It's not deep—so that's good.'

The stewardess arrived with the first aid box and handed it over to him.

'Thanks, Michelle. Are the steps down yet?'

'Yes, sir. We are ready to disembark.'

Marco found a tube of antiseptic cream and some cotton

wool and handed it over to Isobel. 'That should fix you up until you get to the house.'

'Thanks.' Isobel was still trying to pull herself together.

What on earth had just happened? she wondered anxiously. Her heart was pounding as if she had run a long-distance marathon, and she felt shaky and hot inside.

And the worst thing was that feeling of pleasure that had blazed inside her just from the lightest brush of his fingertips. That had never happened to her before with anyone. And the fact that it had happened so easily, with such a casual touch, *with Marco* was horrifying.

That *had* to be in her imagination…

Numbly Isobel followed Marco from the plane. They seemed to be in the depths of the countryside. There was a vineyard to her left, and the regimented rows of vines stretched up as far as the purple haze of the mountains. Straight ahead of them there was an aircraft hangar, which was the only building in the vicinity.

Heat shimmered in a misty, watery illusion—like a stream running across the Tarmac.

That heat haze was like her attraction to Marco, Isobel told herself firmly. It looked real, but it was just an illusion—non-existent. Just because you thought you could see something it didn't mean it was really there.

She glanced over towards him. He was holding the jacket of his suit casually over one shoulder, and he looked extremely relaxed—every inch the Mediterranean millionaire, completely at home amidst the rugged terrain. She would have liked to describe him as pretentious, with his company jet behind him and his staff bringing the luggage out for him, but in all honesty he looked too casually indifferent for that.

She remembered the gentle touch of his fingers against her skin, remembered the heat in his eyes, and her stomach flipped.

What the hell was the matter with her? Hastily she looked

away again. He was Marco Lombardi, one of the most notorious womanisers on the planet, and she couldn't afford to
forget that even for a minute.

There was a car approaching. She could hear the low,
throaty murmur before she saw it, and then a limousine pulled
up from around the side of the aircraft hangar and a chauffeur
jumped out to open the passenger doors for them.

CHAPTER FOUR

THE road from the airstrip out to Marco's villa was a narrow, winding path that seemed to hug the side of the mountain, and every now and then as they rounded a corner there were sheer perpendicular drops down towards the Mediterranean. It was so spectacular that Isobel found herself holding tight to the edge of the seat as vertigo started to set in.

She didn't know what was more nerve-racking—the drive, or the fact that as they rounded corners her body seemed to keep sliding against Marco's. She wished she'd sat opposite to him now, but he'd advised against it, saying that she would see the view better facing forward and also that it helped to ward off any feelings of travel sickness.

Isobel didn't usually get travel sick, but she had to admit that these roads would test the strongest constitution.

'You were right about the coastline being dramatic,' she said as they rounded another corner and she took in an even more amazing view. They were winding their way downwards now, and she could see glimpses of golden beaches and villas tucked away behind lush tropical greenery.

'Yes, it's a lovely part of the world.' He flicked a glance over at her, noticing with amusement how she was desperately trying not to allow her body to fall against his as the car rounded a particularly narrow bend. For a moment his gaze moved lower. She'd left the top buttons of her blouse unfastened and had folded the collar over—probably so that it hid the stain and the tear in the material. But the small change made all the difference to her appearance; her curves were shown to better advantage and she looked less staid…almost sexy.

His phone rang, and impatiently he reached to answer it. He really had more important things to think about than a pesky reporter.

Marco was speaking in French, Isobel realised distractedly, and he was completely fluent, by the sounds of it. 'How many languages do you speak?' she asked him as soon as he had ended the call.

'Five. It helps in business.'

'Really? Wow!' She couldn't help but be impressed. 'I wish I could speak a second language, never mind a fifth! I did French for years at school, but I still struggle to have a conversation in it.'

'You'll have to practise while you are here,' he said with a shrug. 'It's just a matter of usage. When you have to speak it every day it starts to get easier.'

The limousine turned off the road, and Isobel tried to turn her attention away from him and back to what was happening. But it was hard. Because—she hated to admit it—she found him quite fascinating.

Electric gates folded back, allowing them to enter, and they drove along a wide sweeping driveway lined with giant palm trees. The gardens were very well tended. It was probably a full-time job for a team of gardeners, she thought as she looked out at the tropical shrubs and flowers blazing amidst lawns as smooth as a bowling green. They rounded a corner and suddenly a huge sprawling white mansion opened up before them.

It was built on two levels, and encircled by open verandas that looked out over an Olympic-size infinity pool, its blue waters seeming to merge perfectly with the colour of the Mediterranean.

'Nice house,' Isobel remarked. 'Are you sure it's big enough for you?'

Amusement glinted in the darkness of his eyes. 'You know, now you come to mention it, I suppose it is a bit on the small side.'

They pulled to a halt by the front door, and she reached for the door handle and got out before the chauffeur could come around to open it for her.

The heat of the late afternoon was heavy and silent; the only sound was the swish of waves against the shore beneath them. Isobel turned her head and saw a path leading down to a private beach. She also noticed the oceangoing yacht moored at the end of a long jetty.

'Is that another of your toys?' she asked Marco as he stepped out from the vehicle behind her.

He followed her gaze down towards the sea. 'It's a working toy. I use her for business, but also for pleasure. Sometimes it's good to unwind out at sea, away from everything and everyone.'

For a moment as she looked up at him she thought she saw a glimpse of sadness in the darkness of his eyes, as if at times he needed the solace of being alone out at sea. Then he turned and smiled at her, and she realised that the idea was ludicrous. Marco, international jet-set playboy, would never need solace! What was she thinking?

'Come on—I'll show you up to your room.' He turned away from her and led her into the house.

The entrance hall was palatial; it had a huge, sweeping circular staircase, and vast windows that towered above her like the windows of a cathedral. It was all very modern and new in design. 'How long have you lived here?' she asked curiously as she followed him upstairs.

'About two years now.'

'So you bought the house just after your divorce?' She

was finding it difficult to keep up with him because he was striding along the corridor at quite a pace.

'Around that time, yes.' He opened a door and then waited for her to catch up with him, so that she could precede him into the room.

Her eyes widened. It was decorated in shades of cream and turquoise, and was probably the largest and most luxurious bedroom she had ever been in. The bed alone looked as if it would sleep about twelve people, and there was a walk-in closet that was as big as her entire bedroom at home. The skirt, jeans and the few tops that she'd brought with her were going to look very lonely in there, she thought wryly.

'If this is supposed to be the spare bedroom, the master bedroom must be awesome,' she said as she glanced out of the folding glass doors at the veranda and the spectacular view of the sea.

'Come and have a look, if you want,' he invited. 'I'm right next door.'

She looked over and caught the gleam of mischief in the darkness of his eyes. She found herself blushing. 'Eh...no, thanks. I think my article can do without that particular piece of information.'

'Well, don't say I didn't offer.' He laughed. 'OK, I'll leave you to settle in and I'll see you downstairs for dinner in shall we say...?' He glanced at his watch. 'About an hour?'

'Yes...an hour is fine by me.' Isobel tried to sound confidently upbeat about the prospect of dining with him but her nerves were jangling. She really didn't want to have dinner with him, in fact she'd rather have hidden away from him up here until morning—but that was ridiculous. She had to spend time with him in order to get to know him and gather all the information she needed for her article. What on earth was wrong with her? It was just work, she reminded herself sternly.

As Marco left the room the chauffeur brought her suitcase in. Then she was left alone.

For a while she wandered around, investigating her surroundings. The *en suite* bathroom was completely mirrored, and it had a Jacuzzi hot tub positioned so that you could lie and look out on the veranda and the view of the sea. Maybe she'd do that later. Her shoulder was still a little sore, so it might help. But for the time being she decided to make do with bathing the wound and putting on some more antiseptic. As she pulled her blouse back to examine the damage in the mirror, the memory of Marco's hand touching her skin suddenly flared from nowhere. Hurriedly she blanked the memory out. Why did she keep thinking about that?

What she should be concentrating on was her article.

Deciding to busy herself before dinner, she got her pen and notebook and went to sit outside on the veranda.

It was about six in the evening, but the day was still warm and a delicious little breeze rustled through the palm trees. For a while she just sat there admiring the view, thinking back over the day.

Let's see, what do I already know about Marco? she mused. Apart from the fact that he's a ruthless wheeler-dealer.

On impulse, she took out her phone and decided to look on the internet for the name of the company that she had seen on his papers today. What was it…? Porzione…

She typed the name into a search engine and waited, but there was nothing except a charity for disabled children. She glanced at it briefly. It also supported families with premature babies, and did some very good work counselling couples dealing with the death of a child, but it was clearly nothing to do with Marco. Maybe she'd spelt it wrong. She was about to close the box, but before she did so something made her type Marco's name into the mix.

Immediately his name flashed up on screen as the founder

and director of Porzione, and she sat back in her chair. Why would Marco have founded a children's charity?

Curiously she typed in Marco's name followed by just the word *charity*, to see what else came up. To her surprise his name was associated with a very long list of charitable organisations.

Strange how that was never mentioned in the media—but then judging by the way she'd had to search for his name it seemed he liked to keep a low profile. And of course, stories about charities probably didn't sell as well as stories about his love-life.

A curl of guilt stirred inside her. Why hadn't she discovered this before? She drummed her fingers against the arm of the chair as she thought about her findings. A lot of big businessmen donated to charity, she told herself sensibly. And just because Marco donated money to good causes it didn't make him a good person. It was probably some kind of tax dodge, anyway.

She returned her attention to the internet and impulsively typed in the name of his ex-wife—Lucinda White. A lot of information came up about the films she had starred in, but there was also a lot of material about her marriage to Marco.

Isobel glanced through some of the old articles and photographs.

As the couple had always fiercely guarded their privacy, almost everything that was written was pure conjecture. The only fact that couldn't be denied was that they had once loved each other, as evidenced in some of the snatched photographs of them together.

They had made a very glamorous couple, and it was no wonder the press had been obsessed with them. A picture of Marco and Lucinda together at a party or even out for an afternoon stroll had sold newspapers and magazines by the ton. There had been a greedy appetite to know everything there was to know about their whirlwind love affair—where they shopped, where they went on holiday, how they decorated their home in Beverly Hills. In fairness, Isobel could see why Marco disliked the press. It had all got a bit out of hand.

Although the couple had studiously avoided giving the media any intimate details about their lives, people had thought they knew them—thought their relationship was the real thing. They had been depicted as the perfect couple.

Then suddenly, eighteen months later, the marriage had ended without any explanation.

Irreconcilable differences, they'd said. But they hadn't said what those differences were. The divorce had been quick and yet dignified. There had been no war over money, no trading of recriminations or insults—in fact they had stated that they would always be friends.

That had been almost two years ago now, and since the split neither one of them had been involved with anyone else. There had been rumours every time Marco was seen out with a woman—which was frequently. But there seemed to be no one serious in his life, and the same for Lucinda.

Some people said that they still loved each other. But if that were the case they would still be together. It wasn't as if the press interest had diminished because they were divorced. In fact it had sparked a whole new direction of spin.

There were lots of articles on the internet now with various theories about what had happened. Some said Marco had just reverted to type and got bored—once a womaniser always a womaniser, they said. Some alleged that Lucinda had wanted children and Marco hadn't. A few suspected that Lucinda had been the one to have an affair.

So what was the truth? Isobel wondered.

If she had to guess, her money would be on Marco having an affair—possibly the thought of committing to a family had sent him running scared for the hills. You only had to look at the articles and the lists of women he had dated both before and after his marriage to realise he liked playing the field. There were even kiss-and-tell articles by women he had unceremoniously dumped after just a few dates. He was a player. It wasn't rocket science.

But of course she could be wrong, she reminded herself, because she was just guessing. Lucinda was a very beautiful woman and a very successful actress; she *could* have been the one who'd had a fling.

Isobel paused to look at one of her publicity pictures. The actress was wearing a white bikini that left little to the imagination. She had a fabulous body, glorious long blonde hair and big blue eyes.

Maybe one of her leading men had made a play for her and she hadn't been able to resist. Things like that happened all the time in Hollywood.

But if she'd been the one to have an affair wouldn't it have been splashed all over the papers? Since the divorce there had been no rumours about Lucinda, no cosy photographs of her out having dinner at restaurants and then returning to someone's apartment late at night, leaving early in the morning. Not like Marco.

Marco seemed to have sailed through his divorce without giving it a second thought. Although there was one shot of him just after the decree nisi where he looked as if the whole thing had suddenly got to him.

She flicked back to that photograph and studied it. They'd caught him leaving his offices, and there was a bleak look in his eyes, a troubled air about him.

Perhaps he wasn't unfeeling. Perhaps Lucinda had been unfaithful and he had been devastated.

As soon as the thought crossed her mind Isobel frowned. Why was she suddenly looking for excuses for him? He'd probably looked shattered that day because he'd been out all night, or because he hadn't made as many millions that week as he'd expected—not because his divorce was final.

Nevertheless she was supposed to be keeping an open mind,

she reminded herself. If she had to write a celebrity interview, the least she could do was to make it the best interview she could, and that meant being accurate with details.

Isobel sighed and disconnected from the internet. She would find out the truth, she told herself with determination, and she would start by putting some questions to Marco to-night over dinner.

With that thought in mind, she got to her feet and went inside to get ready.

It was strange… She was usually so eager to get a story, and not at all nervous. But as she headed downstairs a little while later her confident business mood felt as if it was evap-orating—a fact that wasn't helped when she rounded a corner and caught sight of her reflection in the hallway mirror. The black skirt and blouse she was wearing were OK for the office, but for dinner with Marco they seemed suddenly lamentably dull.

Isobel frowned. She had interviewed a lot of different people over the years, and this was the first time she had ever worried about what she was wearing! Usually she was totally focused on getting the story. And that was how she should be now, she told herself firmly. It wasn't as if she was out to impress Marco—which was just as well, considering his usual dinner companions were movie stars and models. This was just work.

Trying to forget the stupid undercurrents that were whirring around inside her, she held her head high and moved down the corridor in search of her quarry.

A door was open a little further along, and as she looked in she saw Marco sitting behind a desk in a large book-lined study. He was immersed in paperwork and didn't hear her until she knocked on the door. Then he sat back and smiled.

Something about that lazy, casual smile and the way his gaze drifted over her appearance made her senses start to spin. 'Sorry, I didn't mean to interrupt…'

'That's OK—I'm just finished. Come on in,' he invited.

It entertained him to watch her reactions to him—she was so cautious, like a gazelle poised for flight. And even her dress sense seemed to verge on the side of caution. She looked smart, but in a very efficient, non-sexual way. The black top she was wearing was loose and completely hid her curves. Anyone would think she was scared of allowing a man to look at her body, he thought. And why did she insist on scraping her hair back into a ponytail like that?

Isobel tried to pretend that she didn't notice the analytical way he was dissecting her appearance, but she could feel herself tensing even more. OK, she knew she was not model material, but he had no right to look at her like that!

'So, what are you working on?'

Her voice was deliberately cool and businesslike, and he laughed. 'With a question like that, I take it you're still working as well?'

'Well…that *is* why I'm here.' She tried to angle her head up in a way that told him that she didn't care what he thought about her—that there might be a million women in France who would give anything to be here in his company and would probably dress up for him, but she wasn't one of them. She was totally work-orientated.

To her consternation he just kept looking at her, with that gleam in the darkness of his eyes, as if she were a very interesting sub-species and as if to say, *I know you're not immune to me.*

But that was in her imagination, she warned herself hastily. Maybe he looked at every woman with that same provocative gleam in his eye.

'So, you were telling me what you are working on?' She tried to jog him lightly into continuing.

'I wasn't, actually,' he replied with amusement. 'But seeing as you are enquiring so…nicely…I'll tell you. I'm putting a deal together to buy a French company called Cheri Bon.'

'The name rings a bell...' She frowned. 'Oh, yes—I read about them last year. It's a confectionery company that started out as a small family-run concern and made it big very quickly. Didn't they get into financial trouble because they'd overstretched themselves?'

'Well done.' He looked impressed. 'Obviously all that reading material next to your bed on the financial markets isn't just for show.'

'There is no need to sound quite so surprised. I am a journalist, you know, and we like to keep abreast of what's going on.'

'Ah, yes... So you are...' He smiled. It was strange but every now and then he found himself forgetting that.

'Anyway, I thought you were buying the Sienna confectionery company.' She got the point in quickly.

She was very much the journalist now, he noted as he pushed his chair back from the table to stand up. 'Come on— let's go and have dinner. I've had enough of business.'

'So...are you buying both companies?' Even though she knew she probably shouldn't be asking, she couldn't leave the subject.

He just laughed. 'You're tenacious, aren't you?'

'Just interested.' She shrugged.

'Well, how about I tell you all about Cheri Bon tomorrow?' he suggested nonchalantly. 'They have their main factory in Nice. You can accompany me down there and I will fill you in on my visionary plans for a very sweet future.'

'Really? That would be great!' Her eyes widened with interest. 'So I take it you're hoping to merge the two companies?'

'As I said, I've had enough of business for now. That's tomorrow's subject, Izzy.' He put a hand on her arm and steered her towards the door. 'Now, let's see what Stella has prepared for us to eat.'

The light touch of his hand sent weird little darts of

awareness through her body, and she quickly moved away from him, hoping he wouldn't notice.

But Marco did notice. He also noticed how she deliberately gave him as wide a berth as possible as he stood back to allow her to go ahead of him out of the door. It was as if she was terrified of accidentally brushing against him—in fact of having any bodily contact with him at all. And maybe that unleashed something of the hunting instinct in him, because as he watched her walk past he found himself deliberately wanting to step into her path, hem her in, just so that he could see the light of consternation in her eyes, the pulse beating at the creamy base of her throat.

He forced himself to do no such thing. But as he followed her out and along the corridor, he found his eyes drawn to her hips. He suspected that she had a nice figure beneath those staid clothes, and the more he was around her the more his curiosity was building.

'We're dining outside, Izzy,' he told her as he opened a door into the warmth of the evening.

Isobel found herself out on the terrace. A table had been laid for two, and candlelight flickered and reflected over crystal wine goblets and silver cutlery. There was even an ice bucket that contained a chilled bottle of wine, open and ready for them. The scene looked impossibly romantic against the backdrop of the Mediterranean Sea, now tinged with the oyster-pink of the setting sun.

'You seem to have gone to a lot of trouble,' she murmured apprehensively.

He smiled. 'I haven't gone to any trouble at all, I assure you; this is all the work of my cook, Stella. She always…how is it you English say?…pushes the boat when I have company for dinner.'

'Pushes the boat *out*,' she corrected him absently. 'She does know that I'm not one of your girlfriends, doesn't she?' she added impulsively. 'And that this is a working dinner?'

'No, I don't think she does know that.' She could see a teasing gleam in the darkness of his eyes now. 'Stella is my chef, Izzy. I've never felt the need to furnish her with the personal details regarding my dinner arrangements. Apart from anything else, I don't think she would be remotely interested. However, if you feel it's important I will of course call her out here and bring her up to speed for you.'

'No—no, obviously it's not important.' Isobel could feel herself starting to blush. Why had she said that? Why did she keep feeling the need to assert businesslike boundaries? It wasn't as if Marco would be interested in her in a million years! No wonder he was looking so amused.

In desperation, she tried to salvage her pride. 'It's just that I might need to make notes as we talk, that's all, and if you'd told her she might have laid the table with a bit more practicality. It's a little dark out here...don't you think? With just the candlelight?'

'Ah! I understand.' He pulled out one of the chairs for her and watched as she walked hesitantly over to sit down. 'Well, I'll just have to see what I can do about that for you. There are some extra lights out here somewhere.'

'Thank you.' Why did she feel so unbearably self-conscious? she wondered angrily. Why was she aware of every nuance in his voice, every flicker from his dark eyes as they moved over her?

She watched as he walked across to a light switch and switched it on.

'So how is that?' he asked.

Isobel had expected a bright overhead light to come on, but instead garden lights flickered on, glittering like icicles around the palm trees and the edges of the veranda, giving the gathering dusk an even more romantic feel.

'As you probably know, that isn't any help at all,' she muttered, and he smiled.

'Really? I think it's much better.' ' He strolled back and sat down opposite. 'Best I can do, I'm afraid.'

Somehow Isobel didn't believe him. In fact she got the distinct impression he was enjoying her feeling of discomfiture. 'Well, never mind. I'll just have to use my Dictaphone,' she said as she reached to get it out of her bag. 'You don't mind, do you?' Without waiting for an answer she turned it on and put it down in the centre of the table.

'Actually, yes, I *do* mind.' Calmly he leaned over, picked the machine up and talked into it. 'Note to Ms Izzy Keyes... You need to relax a little, unwind and switch off.' As he spoke his eyes held hers. 'And by the way—has anyone ever told you that you look quite extraordinarily attractive when you are angry?'

Then he switched the machine off, and watched as her green eyes blazed with fire.

'Marco, stop making fun of me! I really need to start assimilating information for my article,' she told him in consternation.

'I wasn't making fun. I was being serious.' And he really was, he realised suddenly. There was something exciting about the way her intelligent green eyes could blaze like that—the way her smooth, pale skin could warm up to boiling point.

'Let's assimilate information the old-fashioned way... hmm?' He murmured huskily. 'Let's have a conversation and get to know each other.' He watched as her eyes narrowed warily on him. 'Anyone would think I'd suggested something scandalous,' he said humorously.

'No, you haven't, but I think you are missing the point.' Her heart was thudding uncomfortably hard against her chest as she strove to sound in control. 'I'm interviewing you, and—'

'No, I think *you* are missing the point Izzy. We are sitting on a terrace overlooking the Mediterranean, about to have dinner. Life is too short for rigid rules. You can assimilate your information, as you like to put it, but let's do it my way.'

'Yes, but—'

'*My* way Izzy…or no way.' He cut across her firmly.

'Well, what can I say…?' She shrugged helplessly. She wasn't at all happy about the way this conversation was going, and she was totally out of her comfort zone now. 'I was just trying to be organized, so I don't forget anything.'

It was strange, but the more she tried to put up her business-like barriers the more Marco felt inclined to tear them down. 'You won't forget anything,' he told her softly. 'And here's a radical idea—if you do, you can ask me in the morning and I'll remind you.'

He leaned across and filled both of their wine glasses.

'Now, what shall we drink to?' he asked nonchalantly.

She wanted to tell him again that she didn't drink while she was working, but as she saw the humour glittering in the darkness of his gaze she realised he expected her to say that. So she changed her mind.

'How about the truth?' she said quietly instead. 'Let's drink to that.'

The suggestion jarred a little with Marco. 'Since when has a journalist ever been interested in the truth?'

'Since right now.' Her eyes held with his, and something about his derisive remark made her lean forward earnestly. 'Not all journalists are the same. We are not all out to sensationalise a story, or get the story at any cost.'

'Nice try, Izzy.' He laughed, but this time there was little humour in the sound. 'But that's not my experience.'

'Well…you obviously just haven't met the right journalists.'

'Is that a fact?' Marco's eyes drifted over her lazily. He couldn't quite work out if she was just the most practised liar in the world, or if that really was sincerity in her voice.

Not that he particularly cared—because, no matter how

much sincerity shone from her, she would not be getting the inside track on his marriage breakdown. There were some things that he would never discuss with anyone, never mind a journalist.

'Well…we'll see.' He shrugged. 'So, why don't you set the conversation rolling and tell me a little about yourself?'

'I think you've just stolen my line.' She cast him a fulminating glare from wide eyes, and he laughed.

'Izzy, if I'm going to tell you about myself, the least you can do is give me a brief summary of your life.' He reached and took a sip of his wine. 'That's the thing I hate about the paparazzi—total strangers shouting questions. What gives them the right…hmm?'

The softly asked question made her look over at him. She supposed he had a point. But even so she was loath to open up to him even on a superficial level. 'I'm really not that interesting,' she murmured.

'I don't believe that for a moment.'

Oh, he was far too smooth, she thought nervously.

Marco noted the shadows in the depths of her eyes. He still couldn't fathom why he found her so fascinating, but he did. Perhaps it was nothing more than idle curiosity…because she certainly wasn't his type. Maybe she just stirred the hunter instinct in him, or maybe it was that air of fragility that gave her a certain mystery.

Whatever it was, he found himself remembering that moment when he had unfastened the top button on her blouse. The intensity of the sensual heat that had flared between them had been quite a surprise.

And as his gaze flicked down over her again he found himself thinking that he would like to unbutton her a little more and then take her to bed—just for the hell of it.

CHAPTER FIVE

DARKNESS had fallen quickly, and there was a full moon shimmering in the inky blackness of the sky, its light reflecting over the stillness of the sea like a wide silver pathway to heaven. There was something very surreal and tranquil about the scene, but there was nothing tranquil about the way Isobel was feeling.

Every time she met Marco's dark gaze across the table she could hear her heart thundering, as if she were running fast across difficult terrain pursued by the devil himself.

Why was that? she wondered distractedly. Was it just the fact that he was undeniably handsome?

The white shirt unbuttoned at the neck seemed to emphasise the smooth olive tones of his skin. His thick dark hair was immaculately groomed. Even the hint of stubble on his square jaw made him look more…enticing…if that was the word she was looking for. She frowned…. Maybe not! She certainly couldn't use that adjective when she wrote about him!

'So, you were about to tell me about yourself?' He smiled, as if her hesitation totally amused him.

'Marco, I really don't see the point—'

'Well, you will just have to humour me, won't you?' He cut across her easily. 'Tell me about your parents and your childhood—that kind of thing.'

She shrugged. 'I was brought up in London,' she began hesitantly. 'And my mother lives in Brighton now.'

'And your father?'

'I don't know where he is. He left when I was eleven and he didn't come back.'

'Not even to see you?' Marco frowned.

'My dad was a bit of a complex character,' she murmured non-committally.

'Which is code for the fact that he was a dreadful parent, I take it?'

It was really strange, but she found she didn't want to tell Marco that he was right. Why was that? she wondered. Was it because she remembered that Marco was the man who had sacked her father from the job he'd loved at the factory? Did she still feel some kind of loyalty towards her dad? The discovery surprised her, because her dad certainly didn't deserve any kind of loyalty after the way he'd behaved... Maybe that old saying about blood being thicker than water was true!

'Let's just say he had problems. Everyone can't get a best parent award, I suppose.' She reached and took a sip of her wine. He was looking at her with that close attention that unnerved her so much—as if he were interested in her—as if he cared about what she was telling him.

He was just practised in that kind of concerned attitude, she told herself quickly. It came under the heading of charm.

But even so, those dark eyes were incredibly warm as they held hers...

They were interrupted by Marco's cook, who came to put some plates of prosciutto on the table, accompanied by ciabatta bread. She was a large lady in her fifties, and obviously couldn't speak much English—because Marco introduced her in French, and the conversation stayed in that language for a few minutes as the woman put some bowls of olives on the table. There was a lot of laughter and what sounded like light-hearted banter, and Isobel was glad of the interlude.

Glad to switch her thoughts away from old memories and the new challenge of not getting drawn in by Marco's smooth charisma.

'Stella says that our starter for this evening is Italian, in my honour, and that our main course is British, in your honour,' Marco told her as they were left alone again. 'But apparently the dessert is French, in honour of the fact that French food is the best—not that she is biased at all.' He laughed.

'No, obviously not.' She smiled. 'She seems a nice lady.'

'Yes, she is—and as a rule she is very reliable... However, all is not as it seems.'

'Oh?' She looked over at him intrigued, thinking he was serious. But then she saw the gleam of humour in his eyes.

'I have a feeling these olives are not truly Italian,' he said seriously. 'I believe they come from a grove down the road.'

'No!' She played along with him and looked suitable horrified. 'That's very underhand of her, isn't it?'

'Absolutely. You can't trust anyone nowadays.' He reached and took one of the plump green olives from the bowl to examine it closely. Then he put it into his mouth.

'So what's the verdict?' she asked with a smile.

'Not so sure I can tell you...' He looked at her with a raised eyebrow. 'I don't want my views splashed all over the papers tomorrow. The olive world in Italy could be in uproar.'

She giggled.

'You may laugh, but we take our food very seriously in Italy.'

'Don't worry—you'll find I am the soul of discretion. Sensitive, responsible journalism is my speciality.'

'Hmm...well, as I said earlier I'll reserve judgement on that for a while.' Their eyes held for a moment. Then he smiled at her and slid the bowl a little closer to her. 'Try one—they are very good.'

They *were* good she thought, as was the warm bread and the prosciutto. She hadn't realised how hungry she was until now. But when she thought about it she hadn't eaten since breakfast.

'So, moving on from your childhood, tell me about the guy who broke your heart?' Marco asked suddenly.

The question took her completely aback. 'What makes you think someone has broken my heart?'

'I don't know. Call it a wild guess.' He shrugged. 'Sometimes I imagine I catch a vulnerable look in your eyes.'

'Sorry to disappoint you, but I'm more your practical, pragmatic type.' She raised her chin.

'The tough journalist, coolly aloof from emotional ties— that kind of thing?' He looked vaguely amused.

'Yes…that kind of thing.'

As their eyes held across the table Marco wasn't sure what he believed about her. There was something about the hesitation in her reply, that expression in her eye…

'And, you know, my love-life really isn't any of your business,' she continued fiercely.

'Ah! But in a few moments you will be asking me about *my* love-life won't you?' he countered. 'You'll be traipsing out all the old tired questions.'

'I don't have any old or tired questions; mine are all fresh and full of zing.'

He laughed at that.

'But actually we *should* move on to that—'

'So you've never been married?' Marco continued lazily, as if she hadn't even spoken. 'Never lived with anyone?'

Why did he keep asking her these personal questions? He was driving her mad. 'I was engaged for a while. But it didn't work out and we called it off.' She slanted him a warning look. 'I'm over it. There's no underlying vulnerability to me whatsoever.'

'And did this happen fairly recently?'

'About six months ago. Now, can we move on?' There was an unconsciously pleading look in her eyes.

'OK, I won't say another word on the subject.' He held up his hands.

'Good—because we are supposed to be talking about you.'

Stella interrupted them to clear away their plates and put out some serving dishes between them.

'I hope you are not going to be disappointed,' Marco said as they were left alone again.

'Why?' She looked over at him with a frown, thinking he was talking about their interview.

'Because your British dish…' he lifted the lid off one of the casserole dishes '…is not roast beef.' He flicked her a teasing look and she couldn't help but smile.

For a while there was silence between them as he put some food onto her plate. 'I think it is beef casserole with herbs of Provence,' he said as he tasted it. 'Which *I* would think is a French dish.'

'Whatever it is, it's very good. I wish I could cook like this.'

She could hear the sound of the sea against the shore beneath them; there was something very relaxing about it, and about the warmth of the air.

She looked down over the garden towards the sea. 'I can understand why you bought this house. The setting is spectacular. But I'm surprised that you have your main home here in France. I would have thought, being Italian, your home would be in Italy.'

'Italy will always be my first love, but I have to admit that I'm torn. France is like a very beautiful mistress—compelling and provocative, hard to get out of the system.'

There was a honeyed edge to his voice that made little darts of adrenalin shoot through her.

'Well, you'd know all about mistresses, I suppose,' she murmured, trying to ignore the sensations.

'I know about passion,' he corrected softly. 'How it can fire the senses, take you over.'

Something about the way he was looking at her made her feel hot inside…made her wonder what it would be like to be kissed by him, to be held in those strong arms. As soon as the thought crossed her mind she was shaken. She had more sense than to ever be attracted to him, she reminded herself furiously.

'So, is that what happened with your marriage?' Desperately she tried to bring herself back to reality by asking the question. 'Did you go out one night and meet someone, and allow passion to take you over to the point where you allowed yourself to forget that you were married?'

'Same old tired questions…' He shook his head. 'And I thought you said you could do better.'

The mocking words made her skin flush with colour. 'It's the question people are interested in.'

'It's two years since my divorce, Izzy. You'd think people would have moved on.'

There was an undercurrent to the words that she couldn't work out. Was it anger? Sadness? Or just plain irritation?

Their eyes held. 'Are you going to give me an answer?' she asked hesitantly, and he shook his head.

'Not right now…no.'

The reply took her by surprise. 'But you invited me here specifically to interview you about your life—'

'My life is more than my divorce, surely?' He fixed her with that mocking look that completely unnerved her. 'I think you should work up to that question.'

'Do you?' She looked at him archly. 'Is this let's-make-the-journalist-jump-through-hoops time?'

He laughed. 'You know, I like the sound of that!'

Stella interrupted them again as she came to clear the table and serve the desert—a *crème brulée* with a thick, creamy crust that Isobel would have enjoyed if she hadn't completely lost her appetite now.

'So, what questions am I allowed to ask you, Marco?' she murmured as they were left alone again. 'I suppose it's OK to dwell on your life in the fast lane, with your planes and your yachts?'

'I thought you said you didn't exaggerate? It's one plane and one yacht,' he corrected her with a smile, and then sat back in his chair to regard her steadily. 'And am I to gather from that note in your voice that you disapprove of my—as you call it—life in the fast lane?'

'It's not my place to disapprove or approve. I'm just making an observation.' She shrugged.

'Oh, is that all it is?' He laughed. 'And your *observation* is that I have no idea what real life is like? Is that it? That I don't know how poverty can bite to the bone?'

She shrugged. 'Well, now you come to mention it—'

'Izzy, I spent the first eight years of my life living in the back streets of Naples. We had nothing.'

She frowned. 'But I thought you came from a wealthy family.'

'My mother was from a wealthy family, but she was cut off without a penny when she married my father because he had committed the ultimate sin of being born poor. It was only when my father died that we were received back into the fold.'

'I didn't know that,' Isobel said in surprise. 'The blurb on your background always says that you are from a wealthy dynasty.'

'Well, there you are, you see—you don't know everything.' Marco's mobile phone started to ring, and he lifted it up to look at the screen. 'Excuse me, I'll have to take this. It's a business call.'

Isobel watched as he leaned back in his chair, noticing how his Italian tones blended attractively into the warmth of the night. His revelations about his family background had surprised her—how was it that no one had found out this information before? she wondered. And what else didn't she know about him?

Stella came over to the table to see if they were finished and to ask if they wanted coffee. Isobel tried to communicate with her in her stumbling French, thanking her for the meal and declining coffee as she was still enjoying the delicious wine.

'Ah, the wine is from Marco's vineyard in Provence,' Stella said in broken English. 'It is good, yes?'

'Très bon,' Isobel replied and then tried to say that she hadn't realised that Marco owned a vineyard.

Unfortunately Stella replied in such rapid French that Isobel couldn't understand a word, so she just nodded as she watched her clearing the table, and then said a quick thank-you in French before she disappeared.

She caught Marco glancing over at her with that amused look in the darkness of his eyes. Probably laughing at her lamentable attempt to communicate. But not everyone was bilingual. Really, the guy was perfectly impossible!

There was also more to him than she had first realised. He'd obviously been through some tough times in his youth, and he was a bit more...*human* than she'd thought he would be. He had quite a good sense of humour, and—

Suddenly Isobel caught herself. What on earth was she thinking? Even if he'd had a harsh upbringing in Italy, he was still the same ruthless man who had practically stolen her grandfather's firm. Not to mention the fact that he was a womaniser—all good reasons for not being drawn in by that playful gleam in the darkness of his eyes.

On impulse she got up from the table and walked to the edge of the terrace. She could see the pool from here, and the shimmering turquoise water looked cool and inviting in the tropical heat.

She listened to Marco's smooth flow of Italian and wondered what he was saying. She needed to find out more about his ruthless side, she reminded herself—needed to keep her senses firmly grounded.

'You were right about one thing, Izzy,' he observed suddenly, and she turned around to see that he had finished his call and was getting up from the table.

'And what is that?'

'Your conversational French needs work.' He smiled at her.

'Thanks for that. I knew you were amused!'

'No, actually I was impressed that you made an attempt. And amused by the fact that you sounded quite cute as you did so.'

'Thanks,' she murmured with embarrassment. 'What you really mean is that I sounded silly.'

'No, that's not what I meant at all. Don't be so hard on yourself.' He strolled back towards her, and something about the way he was watching her with such intensity made her emotions spin.

'Anyway, we should get back to where we were before we got interrupted by your phone call,' she continued swiftly, her mind racing to try and get back into the safety of work mode. 'You were telling me about your childhood.'

'Was I?' He shrugged. 'I think we should move on from that. Maybe you should tell me a little more about yourself.'

'Is this another of your let's-make-the-journalist-jump through-hoops moments?' she asked.

'No, it's more of a let's-relax moment.' He came to a halt beside her. 'It is ten o'clock, Izzy—don't you ever switch off from work?'

'Says the guy who has just taken a business phone call,' she retorted swiftly.

He laughed. 'You're right. Maybe we are both guilty of burying ourselves in work.' His gaze suddenly turned serious.

'My excuse is that I have a lot of people depending on me to get things done, a lot of jobs riding on my decisions. What's your excuse?'

'I don't need an excuse. And I don't know why you keep asking me these questions.'

'Because I'm interested. In fact I'd say I'm as curious about you as you are about me.'

For a few dangerous seconds she could feel his eyes moving over her face and down to the graze along her collarbone.

She remembered how he'd made her feel when he'd reached to unfasten that one little button at the top of her blouse earlier, and as their eyes connected again she could feel the same heat swirling almost violently inside her. Hastily she took a step away from him.

'Izzy, why are you so frightened of letting your guard down?'

The husky way he asked that question made her heart start to thud nervously. 'I'm not frightened of anything!' He was too damn alert; like a heat-seeking missile he seemed to be able to zone in on her vulnerability...on the fact that she found him far too attractive. Desperately she tried to remind herself that she shouldn't be thinking like this... 'And as for your being worried about people's jobs! Frankly, I find that hard to believe.'

He smiled. 'You could win an award for that defence system of yours, do you know that?'

'I don't know what you are talking about!' She would have backed further away from him, but there was nowhere to go. She was penned in now against the wooden rail.

'I'm talking about the fact that you seem to need to hide behind a businesslike attitude at all times. And it seems to be a pretty negative one as well where I'm concerned. Tell me, are you like this with all men, or is it just me?'

The lazily amused question made her temperature soar. 'I just know the truth about you, that's all.' As soon as the words slipped out she desperately wanted to recall them. She didn't want to make this personal.

'Do you care to explain what you mean by "the truth"?'

There was a tense stillness about him, and as Isobel stared up at him she felt her nerves twisting.

'Not really.' Her voice was a mere whisper. 'Marco, I think we should leave things as they are—I think we should call it a night.'

She tried to move past him but he just reached out a hand and caught hold of her arm.

'On the contrary—you are not going anywhere until you enlighten me.'

The touch of his hand against her arm made her heart thud heavily against her chest.

Their eyes clashed, and she knew he wasn't going to let her go until she said something. 'OK, I just…think you are arrogant and…and ruthless in business.' He was looking at her with that impassive look that fired her blood—as if he was not taking anything on board and as if she were just an irksome little reporter talking rubbish. 'You buy companies and strip them of their assets,' she continued, a little more forcefully. 'You play God as you fire people and tear their lives apart.'

'You certainly hold very biased views about me, don't you?' He shook his head lazily.

The observation made her blush. 'The truth is important to me, Marco—I wouldn't say those things without first-hand knowledge to back up the accusations. And I know that when it comes to business you are in for the kill.'

'I'm a businessman. I have to make tough decisions some-times when I take over a company.' He shrugged. 'But as for your accusations that I fire people without thought and tear companies apart—I don't know where you are getting that from.' His eyes were hard for a moment. 'Where possible I try to move people around within my organisation. I'm in the business of building up strong companies, and I employ a hell of a lot of people.'

'You make it sound so reasonable.' She tipped her head up angrily. 'But I know how you use your power, Marco. I know how you can force small companies into selling to you.' The charge fell from her lips with raw emphasis.

He stared into the blaze of her green eyes. 'Izzy, I have never forced anyone into selling to me.'

'Well, now I *know* you are lying.' With determination she held his gaze. 'And I know that because you forced my grandfather into selling his company to you.'

There—she'd said it! She'd confronted him. But even as the words tumbled out she was regretting them.

Her job was on the line here—she needed to get him on side, get her stupid gossipy interview and just leave. And here she was, raking up stuff that no one except her cared a damn about!

'Your grandfather?' Marco frowned. 'What company would that be?'

She shook her head. 'Look, Marco, I've said too much already. We should leave this subject—because you and I will never agree on your business practices.'

But Marco wasn't even listening to her; instead he was looking at her with that intensity that she found so unnerving. 'Keyes…' He murmured her name as he ran it through his memory banks and then shook his head. 'I don't know what you are talking about…' Suddenly his voice trailed away as he remembered the photo on the shelf in her bedroom. He'd recognised the guy. Like a piece in a jigsaw puzzle the name suddenly flashed into his mind. 'Hayes…David Hayes—that was the man in your photograph. Was he your grandfather?'

He watched the telltale flush of colour on her cheekbones.

'Well, well…' He shook his head. 'I bought that company over ten years ago.'

'There are some things you never forget,' she said stiffly. 'He was a decent honest man and you broke him.'

'Is that what you think?' Marco frowned.

'It's what I *know*,' she told him firmly. 'You squeezed him out…the big guy bullying the small trader…until you got the business for next to nothing.'

'That's not how it happened, Izzy,' he said calmly. 'Yes, once I'd ironed out the problems I did get a good deal with that business. It was a very profitable venture. But it was bad management that was your grandfather's undoing, not me.'

She shook her head. 'He told me—'

'I don't care what he told you. I'm telling you the truth.' Marco cut across her briskly. 'For some reason your grandfather trusted a man he'd put in control of the factory, and he ran the place into the ground. My first job when I took over was to sack him.'

Isobel stared at Marco, and for a moment the earth seemed to tilt to a very strange angle.

'He'd been running up debts, not paying bills. The guy was—' Marco stopped as he saw the colour starting to fade from her cheeks. 'Are you OK?'

'Yes.' She tried to hold her head high.

But she wasn't OK, because suddenly she'd realised that for all these years she had blamed Marco for what he had done to her grandfather…and the real culprit had been her father.

Her father had been in charge of that factory!

Why hadn't her grandfather told her the truth? Why had he backed up all the lies her father had told about the ruthless Marco Lombardi? Even as she asked herself the question she knew the answer. Because in those days she had adored her father, had hero-worshipped him, and her grandfather probably hadn't been able to face disillusioning her. He'd been old school: gentle, courteous. And he had loved her very much. In fact he was probably the only person who had ever truly wanted to protect her.

But the fact remained that he had still lied to her, and that hurt. She'd always thought he was the one man in her life that she'd been able to believe in.

The truth was important to her—no matter how painful, she believed it was always best faced.

Silence seemed to shimmer uneasily as she tried to pull herself together.

'My father ran that factory,' she told Marco quietly.

He nodded. 'I've just made the connection. And I'm telling you the truth, Izzy. The guy was a rogue—and that's putting it politely, for your sake.'

'Don't pretend to do me any favours!' Her eyes held angrily with his for a long moment. Then she looked away helplessly. It had been so much easier to believe that Marco was to blame. Part of her still wanted to believe that he was lying to her now. That maybe her father had done nothing wrong. But even as she said the words to herself they didn't ring true.

Her father wasn't the reliable type… *She knew what he was*.

All those years of looking at the situation from the wrong perspective made her feel foolish. She felt as if someone had just opened a window into her life and an arctic breeze was sweeping all her orderly thoughts into chaos.

Marco put a hand under her chin and tipped her face upwards, so that she was forced to look at him. 'You can apologise any time you like,' he murmured softly.

The touch of his hand made her senses swim.

She didn't want to lower her barriers and apologise to him, because it felt far…far too dangerous.

'Yes, well… I might have got it wrong.' She wrenched herself away from his touch.

'There is no *might* about it. You *did* get it wrong.'

'But the fact still remains that you got a damn good deal when you bought that business,' she maintained stubbornly.

'And since when has that been a crime?' The quietly asked

question sent ripples of consternation though her. 'Izzy, it was over ten years ago, I was just starting out. I saw a business opportunity and I took it.'

Isobel swallowed hard, appalled that she had made such an error. 'OK, I...I made a mistake.'

His gaze raked over her with almost ruthless strength as he took in the fierce glitter in her green eyes.

'And I'm sorry.' The words broke from her lips with trembling force.

She didn't even realise that she was crying until he reached and wiped a tear from her cheek.

'Don't!' She flinched away from the light, disturbing touch of his fingers. 'I feel enough of a fool as it is. And I'm not crying...' She glared at him defensively. 'I'm just angry with myself for getting things so wrong.' She bit down on her lip. 'It all happened before my dad left us, and I still believed in him. I guess my grandfather didn't want to break that.'

'I can understand that,' Marco said quietly.

'Can you? I'm not so sure I can right now.' She brushed a hand impatiently over her face. 'I think he should have told me the truth. Because a few months after his death, when it was apparent there was nothing of value in his will, my father left.'

'And hindsight is a wonderful thing...' Marco said with a shrug. 'Everyone makes mistakes, Izzy. Your grandfather did what he thought was right at the time. He must have loved you a lot.'

The words made her eyes brim with tears again. 'Sorry.' Furiously she tried to wipe them away. 'I'm being stupid.'

'No, you're not.' He looked at her with that teasing gleam in the darkness of his eyes. 'Maybe earlier, but not now.'

The fact that he was being so understanding made her stomach tie into knots as she looked up at him.

And then suddenly his gaze moved towards her lips, and the

atmosphere between them altered subtly, becoming charged with electricity.

'Sorry… Anyway, I suppose we should call it a night, shouldn't we…?' She looked away from him in confusion. She could almost feel the tension crackling between them like a living entity—could feel her heart thundering against her chest as she fought with herself not to sway closer.

What was the matter with her? she wondered frantically.

'Running away, Izzy?' he taunted.

'No! Why should I run away?' Her eyes flicked back towards his and he smiled.

'Good question.' He reached out and idly stroked a finger along the side of her face. The feeling made little darts of awareness shoot through her, and she felt almost drugged by desire as his gaze raked over her lips again.

She wanted him to kiss her, she realised suddenly as he leaned closer…wanted it so much that her whole body ached. The knowledge shocked her, and she told herself to move away from him, but for some reason she couldn't make herself.

'Marco…' She murmured his name softly, and almost as if he were responding to an invitation his lips captured hers.

But this was no ordinary caress. His mouth was skilled, hungry and demanding, and yet so provocative that she was held immobilised by it for seconds.

And then to her consternation she kissed him back, with equal passion. She could taste the salt of her tears against the power of his lips, and she was conscious of thinking that the taste was probably very apt—because she was kissing a man who was experienced in seduction and heartbreak, and she was asking for trouble if she didn't pull away right now and put a stop to the madness.

But it felt so good that she didn't want it to stop. She could feel the warmth from his caress sweeping all the way through her, stirring up a deep longing to be even closer.

If this was how pleasurable it was to be kissed by him, how

would it feel to be even closer? she wondered recklessly. To have his hands against her naked body, holding her, stroking her?

The thought brought fire thrusting through her, and the jolt of it helped her to pull away.

'What are we doing?' She stared up at him in consternation, her breathing ragged as she strove for control.

'I think it's called kissing, Izzy.' He smiled, and unlike her he sounded totally at ease.

'And I think it's called madness. I'm not your type, Marco, and you certainly aren't mine.'

'And yet we seem curiously drawn to each other. '

The matter-of-fact words were like an incendiary device as far as Isobel was concerned, and she shook her head angrily. 'I'm not drawn to you at all!'

'Izzy…Izzy, what am I going to do about you? You are such a bad liar.' The taunting words made her blood boil.

But as their eyes held she knew he was right. She *was* drawn to him. She knew for Marco this was probably just idle curiosity, because she was so far removed from his usual type, but she wasn't sure what it was for her. All she knew was that if he kissed her again the same thing would probably happen—only the next time she might not have the strength to pull away.

The knowledge made panic spin through her.

'Marco, I think under the circumstances I should leave tomorrow and some other reporter from the *Daily Banner* should take my place.'

She really hadn't planned to say the words, they'd just spilled out, and Marco gave a long low whistle. 'You really are scared of me, aren't you?' he reflected softly.

'No! I'm not scared of anything!' She glared at him. 'I'm just trying to be sensible. Everything is getting too personal— and I'm not talking about the…kiss, I'm talking about the link to my past—everything.'

Marco shrugged and moved away from her. 'OK, if you want to leave that's fine. I'll get my chauffeur to drop you at the airport in the morning, But once you leave here, Izzy, my deal with the *Banner* is done.'

'You don't mean that,' she countered.

He met her eyes steadily. 'I always mean what I say, Izzy,' he assured her quietly. 'Always.'

CHAPTER SIX

Isobel couldn't sleep. The night was hot, and her thoughts were racing around in circles, causing her to toss and turn in the huge double bed.

She couldn't understand why she had felt the way she had when Marco had kissed her.

He might not have torn her grandfather's business apart, but he was still a ruthless womaniser, she reminded herself fiercely. He was still the type of predator who could sense weakness and turn it to his own advantage…both in business and in his private life.

So the sooner she got out of here in the morning and returned home to sanity the better.

Isobel turned her pillow around, searching for some cool cotton against her skin and some sleep.

And yet…her brain wouldn't switch off. Because how would she know these facts about Marco were true if she didn't stick around to find out? She'd made a mistake about him once—she didn't want to do it again.

The only thing that she was sure of about Marco was that he was a far more complicated character than she had ever imagined.

That and the fact that he turned her on more than any other man she had ever met.

The knowledge made her temperature shoot through the ceiling, and she tried desperately to block the thought out.

But as she closed her eyes the memory of that kiss returned with powerful intensity, and the fact remained that no man had ever made her feel so alive…or so scared.

Certainly Rob had never set her heart racing like that; in fact he had never unleashed *any* wild feelings of desire. She'd told herself that was what she wanted. That she didn't want to lose control—that she wanted a safe, steady relationship where she could settle down and start a family.

Little had she known that all the time Rob had been pursuing her he'd had another woman in the background. She might never have found out either, if she hadn't called round to his flat late one night after finishing work.

He'd tried to tell her that the scantily clad blonde in his living room didn't mean anything to him—that it was a one-time-only mistake and that it was Isobel's fault for not sleeping with him.

For a while she'd started to wonder if that was true. She'd even started to think that there might be something wrong with her. Because it had always been far too easy for her to pull away from a kiss and to put work first… Easy until now.

The knowledge blazed with unwelcome intensity as she remembered just how difficult she had found it to pull away from Marco.

And she supposed she'd put her job on the line by telling him she wasn't going to continue with their interview. If she went back to the *Daily Banner* without the story they wanted, her reputation would be in tatters.

Her stomach lurched crazily at the thought.

Of all the people in the world to have this effect on her! Why Marco? She couldn't understand it, because he was everything she'd always said she didn't like in a man.

She wondered what he would say if he knew that she was still a virgin. For a moment she imagined his lips twisting in that mocking smile of his. He'd probably tell her she was emotionally scarred from her childhood. He'd been trying to tell her something like that earlier, at dinner.

Angrily she closed her eyes and tried to concentrate on something else. It didn't matter what Marco would say. She didn't care what he thought. And she wasn't scarred from her childhood—if anything, what had happened to her had made her stronger, had taught her to be wary. And there was nothing wrong with that. Especially around someone like Marco Lombardi.

Isobel was just drifting off to sleep when she heard a noise that sounded like a door closing. Frowning, she sat up and listened. But the night was silent.

On impulse she threw the covers back and went over to look out of the window.

The full moon was clear and bright in the sky, and it shone over the curve of the bay, highlighting Marco's yacht moored by the jetty as if someone was shining a spotlight on it.

Isobel glanced at her watch. It was four in the morning. She'd probably just imagined the noise; it was far too early for anyone to be up and about. She was about to go back to bed when she saw Marco, walking away from the house. He was dressed in a suit and he was walking down the path towards his yacht, his steps purposeful.

You didn't dress like that to go for an early-morning sail! Was he taking her at her word and leaving her here to pack up her stuff while he sailed off on business?

It seemed very likely. He'd probably left his chauffeur instructions to drive her to the airport.

The idea sent a wave of panic rushing through her, and she realised suddenly that she wasn't ready to walk away from Marco yet. Not when there was so much more that she needed to find out.

Without even stopping to think about it, she snatched up her dressing gown and went running after him.

When she reflected on the moment afterwards she realised

she hadn't really been thinking straight. All she'd wanted to do was catch up with him and tell him she had changed her mind. Even when she'd stepped outside the front door into the early-morning darkness and realised she hadn't got anything on her feet, it still hadn't made her stop.

It wasn't until she reached the end of the garden path and the start of the long wooden jetty that she paused for breath. The yacht looked much larger and more impressive up close. Giant masts towered above her into the bright starlit sky. This was more like a cruise liner than a private vessel; it was the luxurious toy of a man who only had the best of everything. The kind of pleasure craft where Marco probably entertained sophisticated women-friends—women who would wear cocktail dresses and diamonds—and here she was just in a robe.

For the first time she wondered if this was a good idea. Maybe she should go back to the house, wait for daylight, and then tell the chauffeur that she had changed her mind about leaving.

But say he insisted on following Marco's instructions. Or told her Marco wouldn't be back for a few days.

The thought made her step onto the gangplank and then down onto the polished deck. Apart from the moonlight she was completely in the dark, and it felt slightly eerie. The only sound was the gentle whisper of the breeze in the rigging, and the creak of the ropes that held the ship securely to her mooring.

Isobel stood for a moment, indecisively wondering which way to go, and then to her relief a light flicked on from a window further down.

She headed towards it and peeked cautiously in.

Modern chandeliers blazed over a large lounge area, with white leather sofas and glass tables. But there was no sign of Marco.

Cautiously she walked further down the deck, looking for a doorway, and then suddenly as she rounded a corner there he was—leaning against the rail of the ship, staring out to sea. She didn't realise that he was on the phone until he spoke to someone.

'So, you'll need to prepare those figures for me,' he was saying decisively. 'And I'll head out to New York to deal with it when I can.'

As she moved forward he turned and saw her. 'Anyway, I'll leave it with you, Nick, and phone you later,' he said as he hung up.

For a second there was silence between them as his eyes swept over her, taking in everything about her from her bare feet to the way the black satin dressing gown was tightly belted at her waist.

'Well, now, look what the tide has washed in,' he murmured, and something about that husky tone made her senses plunge into freefall. 'What are you doing out here, Izzy?'

What *was* she doing here? she wondered. She felt suddenly as if she had walked straight into a danger zone. 'I…I couldn't sleep, and then I saw you leaving the house.' She shrugged helplessly.

'You couldn't sleep?' One dark eyebrow lifted.

'No, and I thought I'd better come after you to tell you that I'd changed my mind.'

He moved closer to her. 'Changed your mind about what?'

Her heart seemed to bounce unsteadily against her chest. 'About…our interview, of course.' To her annoyance her voice came out as little more than a whisper. 'I've…I've decided to stay.'

'Ah.' He smiled at that. 'Of course you've decided to stay. You're a journalist—you want your story. I never had any doubts about that. But why are you out here now?'

'I told you…I just thought I'd better come after you in case you'd taken me literally and were going off on business somewhere.' She tried to sound practical, but it was a bit difficult when she was standing in front of him just wearing a dressing gown.

'I *am* going off on business. I've got an early-morning meeting over in Italy. But I was planning on returning to take you down to Nice afterwards.' His eyes narrowed on her. 'You thought I was leaving without saying goodbye?'

'No! Well…yes.' Her voice shook a little. 'As I said, I just wanted to check things were still OK between us after our conversation last night.'

'Yes, things are still OK.' The quiet way he said that, combined with the way his eyes were moving over her face, made her temperature sizzle.

And she realised that her interview wasn't the main reason she'd come running after him. In fact her motivations were somehow much more personal…and for the first time in her life work was on a very low flame by comparison.

The knowledge scared her. 'Anyway, I'll get back on dry land now we have that sorted out…'

'Bit late for that.'

'How do you mean?' Even as she waited for his answer she felt the ship swaying, and her eyes widened.

'The crew have cast off. We are moving out to sea,' he informed her nonchalantly.

'You *are* joking!' In consternation she sidestepped him and headed towards the rail.

But Marco wasn't joking. As soon as she walked out from the sheltered section where they had been standing a warm salt breeze swept her hair around her face. And as she looked out she could see they were a few miles out from land and starting to gather pace.

'Marco, we need to turn back!' she wailed in agitation.

'I haven't got the time to go back, *cara*.'

'But…I can't go to Italy with you!' She turned to face him and then wished she hadn't—because he was standing very close to her…perhaps too close.

'Why not?' he asked with a smile.

'Because…I'm just wearing a dressing gown! Because…' She trailed off helplessly. 'There are a million reasons why not.'

He looked at her quizzically. 'And yet you came running out here without a second thought for any one of those million reasons.'

His gaze drifted slowly over her. She looked totally different with her dark hair loose and tousled by the sea breeze, and he couldn't help comparing her appearance now with the buttoned-up way she usually dressed.

Her black satin dressing gown had slipped down, so that he could see the creamy line of her shoulder and the dark bruise where she had hurt herself on the flight.

He remembered how he'd felt when he'd unbuttoned her blouse. He'd suspected that underneath all that prim clothing she would be a very sexy woman, and the more he was around her the more he realised he was right. That kiss last night, for instance, had been filled with smouldering passion. But for some reason she was afraid of stepping out from behind that cool pretence and letting go.

'You don't understand, Marco. I…I really need to go back.' She tilted her chin and looked up at him with eyes that shone bright and clear in the moonlight.

He couldn't help thinking there was something very touching about the picture she presented.

'I do understand, Izzy,' he told her softly. 'But you've got to understand it's too late to go back.'

The ship rolled and pitched suddenly, and he put a hand out to steady her, catching her around the waist.

She tried to pull away, but the touch of his hand was like fuel to the fire that was suddenly smouldering inside her.

'There is a chemistry between us that can't be denied, Izzy, and you can't keep fighting it.'

'I don't know what you mean.' She raised her eyes towards

his and then immediately wished she hadn't, because he was looking at her with that teasing warmth that made her emotions stretch as if they were made of elastic and were being pulled…pulled to breaking point.

'You know exactly what I mean.' His gaze rested on her lips and she moistened them nervously. 'And I don't think these feelings are going to go away, Izzy, do you? Not unless we address them.'

The calm question rebounded inside her like some instrument of torture.

'You know, I think you are probably *the* most arrogant person I've ever met—and the most infuriating.'

He smiled, liking the fire in her voice, in her eyes. He wondered if she would be as fiery in bed.

Maybe it was time he found out. Because this swirling need that was building between them couldn't be ignored for much longer. It was like an elephant in the room—they both knew it was there, and they both knew exactly what was going on.

And the more she tried to fight against it, the more intrigued he became.

His gaze moved slowly down over her body as he remembered how good it had felt to kiss her last night.

OK, she was a reporter and not his type, but the more he was around her the less it seemed to matter. Well…it didn't matter now, for a few hours, he corrected himself quickly.

He had some time to pass…*why not while it away pleasurably?*

'And do you know *why* I infuriate you so much, Izzy?' he asked softly.

Her heart-rate was starting to increase. Of all the men in the world, why did it have to be Marco who had this effect on her? Why, as soon as he got too close, as soon as he looked at her in a certain way, did she start losing her sanity? She didn't want to lose control…she mustn't lose control, she told herself angrily.

With difficulty she tried to focus. 'The reasons why you annoy me are so…so many, I couldn't possibly begin to list them.'

'Well, let me help you, *cara*… The fact is, I drive you mad because I turn you on.'

The husky matter-of-fact words merged with the surge of the ocean and the hissing of the seaspray as it hit the ship.

She stared up at him, wide-eyed. 'That's…not true…' She tried desperately to insert some fierceness into the denial, but her voice sounded as frail as she suddenly felt. She couldn't believe he had just said that to her!

'You want me to kiss you… And you want me to make love to you… And it scares the hell out of you,' he continued evenly.

She shook her head. 'You are so damn sure of yourself, aren't you?' Her voice trembled alarmingly.

He put one hand on her arm and pulled her closer. 'I'm sure of this.'

Desperately she tried to resist, but he pulled her into his arms with ease, and the impact of his powerful body against hers sent her senses reeling.

She told herself that she needed to pull away, but somehow she couldn't find the strength, and as she looked up at him she was completely terrified by the feelings that were flowing through her.

'Please…Marco…' She whispered the words unsteadily.

'Please…what?' he asked teasingly. 'Please kiss me? Please show me what I've been missing?'

She could feel her heart pounding hard against her chest as he bent closer.

He said something in Italian, and then his mouth captured hers.

For a moment she tried very hard not to kiss him back, but it was like trying to hold a tidal wave at bay. The sensations that were spiralling through her just swept her away. One instant her hands were flat against his powerful chest, and the next they were curling up and around his shoulders as she hungrily kissed him back.

She could taste the salt of the sea on his lips, and the thundering, pounding sound of the ocean seemed to match the pounding of her emotions. *She wanted him so much!*

Just when she thought she couldn't stand it any more, when she thought she would just die from need, she felt his hands untying the belt that held her robe in place.

Her eyes moved to lock with his.

She was naked beneath, and she knew she should reach out and stop him, but she couldn't make herself. Because she wanted him to touch her more intimately—wanted to give herself to him completely.

At first his hands just rested at her waist as he brought her even closer against him, then they smoothed down over her slender hips.

'So, was I right,' he murmured provocatively against her ear. 'You want me so badly it hurts, doesn't it?'

Under ordinary circumstances the words would have infuriated her. She would have slapped him, she would have pulled back, she would have told him to go to hell. But she couldn't do anything rational because a devil seemed to have possessed her senses. She was totally incapable of anything except kissing him, luxuriating in his caresses.

His hand moved from her hips to between her legs. There was nothing tentative about his caress. It was boldly assertive…and the contact of his fingers against such a sensitive area shocked her so much she gasped.

But she liked it… And as he started to caress her *she liked it too much*. She shuddered with need as his mouth captured hers again, his tongue mimicking his fingers, invading her senses and taking over her mind, until she couldn't think about anything except here and now and wanting him.

Then suddenly he pulled away from her. Her breathing was

ragged and uneven and she couldn't get it under control—just as she couldn't stop the pounding need that was still flowing through her body.

'I think we should take this somewhere a little more comfortable, don't you?' he said softly.

She felt dizzy as she looked up at him, and she wasn't sure if that was due to the need he had stirred up in her, or if it was the tilt and flow of the ship as the vessel skimmed through the darkness.

From somewhere a little voice of reason tried to tell her to say no, to walk away. But it was like a voice trying to whisper down a tropical storm—a voice drowned out by the fierce elements of Mother Nature.

He bent and kissed her again, and hunger lanced through her. OK, this was madness, but maybe if she slept with him these feelings would leave her…maybe she would be free of needing him for evermore?

Marco didn't even wait for her acquiescence. He swept her up into his arms and carried her along the deck.

Her heart was thundering out of control as he opened the door into a cabin and placed her down.

She stared up at him, her eyes wide, her silky hair dishevelled around her shoulders, and Marco thought that he had never seen a woman as lovely.

Shyly her eyes moved away from him and around their luxurious surroundings, to linger on the massive double bed.

How many other women had Marco seduced in here? The thought flicked through her mind in a moment of sanity, like a glimpse of clear sky in the midst of a storm. It wasn't too late to say no—to tell him that this wasn't what she wanted.

Except that it was what she wanted. Had been from almost the first moment she'd seen him. He was right.

Marco had taken his jacket off and was unbuttoning his shirt now. He had the most incredible body, she thought hazily.

Powerful, wide shoulders, a hard flat stomach and lean hips. The body of an athlete.

He looked over and caught her watching him, and smiled. 'Come here,' he demanded.

For a moment she hesitated and stood where she was by the door.

'Come.' He stretched over and playfully pulled her closer. Then he sat down on the end of the bed and slid the robe she was wearing down from her shoulders, so that it crumpled to the floor by their feet and she stood before him naked.

'I've been wanting to do that from the first moment I saw you out there on the deck,' he told her huskily.

She felt her body burn as his eyes moved slowly and provocatively over her figure, assessing her with a passionate intensity that made her shyly discomfited whilst at the same time alive with desire.

'Now, wasn't this a good idea?' He whispered the words as he pulled her down onto his knee.

'I don't know…I think I've taken leave of my senses,' she murmured softly as she wrapped her arms around his shoulders. She loved the feel of her breasts pressing against his chest, naked skin against naked skin… 'But I suppose you are used to that…I suppose that is the effect you have on every woman you take to bed…'

He laughed. 'A gentleman doesn't talk about his previous conquests…you should know that.'

'Hmm… Yes, I should know that…' She raked her hands through the thick darkness of his hair and then drew her breath in on a gasp as he kissed her neck, then moved lower to kiss her breasts. 'I also know that you are no gentleman.' She breathed the words out in a wave of pleasure as his lips nuzzled against her nipple. She'd never experienced such breathtaking sensations; she wanted more—was greedy for more. How come no one had ever made her feel like this before? It was as if she were coming alive for the first time.

She bent and kissed his neck, biting him gently.

'And I knew for all that buttoned-up pretence that you'd be a wildcat.' He laughed and rolled her over, straddling her.

She was hardly even listening to him. All she could think about was how much she wanted him. And as his kisses became fiercer, more demanding, she met them gladly, giving herself to him and to the moment totally. They rolled over again, play-fighting as he pretended to try and hold her still.

'Ow!' She winced slightly as he caught her sore shoulder, and instantly his touch gentled and he leaned down to kiss the bruising.

Something about that moment made her want to cry.

She wrapped her arms around him. She liked his superior strength, liked the way he'd placed her, the way he knew exactly how to turn her on, exactly how to tease and torment her. But most of all she liked his tenderness.

For the first time in her life she felt like a woman—could feel the power she had over him. And at the same time she loved the overwhelming control he had over her. It still scared her…but she wasn't going to fight it….couldn't fight it.

Marco reached for the packet of condoms in his bedside cabinet.

'Better safe than sorry…hmm?' he murmured light-heartedly as he rejoined her on the bed.

His lips covered hers, and hungrily she returned his kisses.

It was only when he started to enter her that she froze and gave an involuntary exclamation of pain. Instantly he stopped, and looked into her eyes. 'Am I hurting you?'

'No!' she lied fervently, wanting him to continue, wanting the moment to pass.

He moved against her again, and she bit down on her lip. He *couldn't* find out that she was a virgin—that would be too embarrassing.

Marco pulled away from her with a frown. 'What's the matter?'

'Nothing. Why are you stopping?'

'I'm stopping because I'm obviously hurting you. Anyone would think you hadn't done this before…' His voice trailed away, and she could almost hear his mind ticking over.

'Don't be silly.' She reached up and stroked her hand along the broad contour of his shoulder, willing him to continue, but she couldn't look him in the eye.

He frowned.

No, she couldn't be a virgin, he thought derisively as he remembered the fire and the passion of her earlier responses. But then he found himself remembering other things…the way the chemistry between them had so obviously freaked her out. The way she'd tried to fight against it. The way she had sometimes looked at him as if she were scared of him.

'Isobel, are you a virgin?'

He sounded so incredulous that she felt her whole body suddenly turn cold with indignity. 'No!'

He knew in that one instant that she was lying. He sat up, and as she tried to wriggle away from him pulled her back.

'Isobel, stop it.' He pinned her down easily against the bed with just one hand. The other he used to turn her face, so that she was forced to look at him.

He asked the question again. 'Are you a virgin?'

'What difference does that make?' she blazed, her eyes on fire as they met with his.

'It makes a big difference.' He breathed the words softly. 'Believe me. If you'd told me, I'd have…' He hesitated for a moment.

'You'd have what? Had a good laugh at my expense? Taken pleasure in notching a virgin onto your crowded bedpost?' She cut across him fiercely, his hesitation hurting.

'I'd have taken more care of you,' he said quietly.

'Well, I don't want you to take care of me. This is just sex—no big deal.' Her eyes glittered, over-bright.

Was she trying to convince herself of that, or him? Marco wondered. He stroked her hair tenderly back from her face.

Sex obviously *was* a big deal for her. And someone had obviously hurt her a lot in the past. Who? he wondered. Her father? Or the guy she'd been engaged to? Maybe both?

He told himself that it was none of his business, that he only wanted a light-hearted roll in the sack. But he found himself cradling her against his chest. Then he kissed her again—kissed the tears away from her cheeks.

Hell, but she was so gorgeous…so feminine, so soft…so desirable. Amazing to think that such a body was completely innocent.

But how could he take her now, knowing what he knew?

'Sex *is* a big deal, Isobel.' He whispered the words against her ear. 'And I don't want to hurt you.'

'You won't hurt me,' she murmured, just wanting him to continue.

He drew back from her and looked into her eyes. 'I mean I don't want to hurt you emotionally…'

She frowned, the words causing a curl of sensation inside her that she couldn't even begin to understand.

He stroked a hand tenderly through her hair. 'The thing is I can't make you any promises, *cara*.'

The husky words made her frown, and there was an expression in his eyes that she couldn't begin to fathom.

'You're a player, I know…' Her voice sounded unsteady even to her own ears.

For a second he seemed lost in his own thoughts.

She had the opportunity to pull away, and she told herself that she should. But the fact that he was being honest with her somehow meant something. She'd rather that than lies.

'I don't need any promises, Marco.' She whispered the words softly. 'I just want honesty, and if tonight is all we have then that's fine.'

CHAPTER SEVEN

ISOBEL stretched languorously in the large double bed. Her body felt strange…achy…tired… And yet alive with feelings that just made her want to smile. Why was that? In the moments between waking and sleeping she couldn't think clearly—she wasn't even sure where she was as she rolled over in the bed and reached out into the space next to hers. It was only when she heard herself murmur Marco's name that her eyes jolted open.

What had she done? Even as she was asking herself the question memories were falling in on her—memories that caused such complete and utter panic that she hardly dared look across at the space next to hers.

She held her breath and quickly glanced, but Marco wasn't there. Holding the sheet firmly across her body, she forced herself to sit up and look around the room. He wasn't in the cabin either—she was quite alone.

Relief mixed with overwhelming consternation as she fell back against the pillow. She could hardly believe what had happened, or how easily she'd fallen into Marco's arms last night. She remembered kissing him as they'd stood together out on the deck—she remembered the wild pleasurable sensations, the feeling that it had all seemed somehow to be right, as if she had found a place that she belonged.

She stared up at the ceiling, trying to get her thoughts and her emotions under control. Every woman Marco kissed probably felt like that, she told herself angrily. The man was a master at seduction!

How had she allowed herself to fall for him? The question pounded through her, but as much as she searched there was no rational answer. It was as if she had been somehow bewitched—as if she didn't even know the person she had turned into. One moment she had been trying to cling on to sane and sensible thoughts, and the next...

Memories flooded back—memories of Marco sweeping her off her feet and carrying her down to this cabin—memories of him discovering that she was a virgin.

She groaned and rolled over, burying her face in the pillow. That should have been her wake-up call; she should have called a halt to things right there and then. But she hadn't wanted to!

And even now, as she thought about what had happened next, she felt a strange melting sensation deep inside. At first he had been so gentle with her, easing her through the moment of pain until she'd found enjoyment, and after that he'd seemed to glorify in awakening her body, sending her senses spinning, making her beg for more as he took her to dizzying heights of pleasure over and over again.

Her total lack of control horrified her. She'd always been so adamant that it wouldn't happen to her, but it had—and with Marco Lombardi of all people!

She'd even told him that it was OK if their night together was a one-off. And the strange thing was that she had meant it. She had wanted him so much that the only thing that had mattered was the moment.

A wave of red-hot heat enveloped her body, and hastily she flung the covers back and got out of bed.

It was best not to dwell on it, she told herself fiercely. OK, it was one night of madness. But people did that in today's modern world. It was no big deal because it would never happen again.

Somehow the words didn't make her feel any better.

But it was best forgotten, she told herself again. She was sure Marco had forgotten it already, moved on to something more important. The ship didn't seem to be moving, so they were probably at anchor somewhere in Italy and he was probably in some boardroom somewhere, his mind totally focused on his work. Sex, to a man like Marco, was just recreation—business was all-important. She should be the same.

Isobel headed for the *en-suite* bathroom, turned on the shower and stepped under its full forceful jet. She would concentrate on work now too, she told herself sensibly, and hopefully this time when she sat opposite Marco and tried to question him about his life all those undercurrents of sensual tension would be gone—played out—exhausted.

It was the modern way.

Desperately Isobel tried to ignore the little tremor of consternation at the thought of sitting opposite him again—at the thought of trying to behave as if nothing had happened between them.

She could do it, she told herself sternly—she *had* to do it. Because last night had been just meaningless sex, and to think of it in any other way would be a grave mistake.

Stepping out of the shower, she reached for a towel and wrapped it around her body. Marco's shaving gear was on the side of the hand basin, and she remembered suddenly how roughly abrasive his skin had been against hers last night—how somehow the feeling had been incredibly erotic.

She remembered how his kisses had moved lower down over her abdomen, then lower still, until her body had seemed to liquefy into pleasure.

Swiftly she shut the thoughts away and headed back to the bedroom. She couldn't afford to think about how much she'd enjoyed last night—not when she had to face Marco in a professional capacity today. Things were difficult enough—

especially as she had no clothes to wear except the robe from last night.

Reluctantly she picked the dressing gown up from the floor and put it on. As she did so she glanced at the clock on the bedside table.

It was a shock to find that it was almost midday!

She wondered if Marco was still at his meeting or if she would find him up on deck casually having lunch. The very thought made her nerves twist unbearably, and she glanced in the mirror to check her appearance.

She didn't look her best. Her skin was flushed, and her lips were slightly swollen from Marco's kisses, plus her hair was starting to dry in curls around her face. But who cared? she told herself firmly. She wasn't trying to impress. Marco meant nothing to her. *Nothing.* And she wasn't going to be one of those women who imagined she could change him—or that one night with him somehow meant something. That would be taking the stupidity of what she had done to the absolute limit.

Gathering her courage, she opened the door and headed up towards the deck to investigate.

The day was bright and warm, and the sky was a clear azure blue. Taking deep breaths of the sea air, she looked around. They were anchored in tranquil waters a little way out from the coastline, and she could see the colourful blaze of a busy harbour in the distance against a backdrop of mountains.

As she walked further along the deck she came to a dining area with a table set for one. The white linen tablecloth and silver cutlery gleamed in the sunlight.

'Good morning, *mademoiselle*.' A man of about her own age dressed in a smart black uniform came up from the galley. 'Are you ready for breakfast?' he asked as he walked over to pull out the chair for her.

The polite request took her aback somewhat—this was like being in a five-star hotel, she thought.

'Just coffee would be good, thank you.'

'Are you sure I can't get you something more? Scrambled egg…cereal…croissants? Monsieur Lombardi said you were to make yourself completely at home.'

'That's very kind, but just coffee, thank you.' She sat down at the table and watched as he went to pick up a silver coffee pot that was sitting on a side table. 'Where is Mr Lombardi this morning?' she asked, trying to sound casual, as if she didn't really care.

'He is attending a business meeting in Nice, *mademoiselle*.'

'Nice?' Isobel glanced towards the coast. 'I thought we were in Italy.'

'We were in Italy earlier this morning, *mademoiselle*, but now we are back in France.'

At least Marco wasn't on the ship. She relaxed a little at the knowledge. You see, she told herself firmly. Business came first with Marco, and that was exactly how *she* should be.

The rich aroma of coffee mingled with the warmth of the sea air as the waiter poured her coffee. 'The morning papers have been delivered, *mademoiselle*,' he said as he replaced the pot back down on the table beside her. 'And also a parcel for you. Would you like me to bring them to the table?'

'Yes, please.' She watched, intrigued as he disappeared down to a lower deck. The parcel probably wasn't for her at all—it was probably for another one of Marco's girlfriends. After all, nobody knew she was here so it couldn't be for her!

The waiter returned with a stack of papers and two gold boxes wrapped with red ribbon.

'So, were these delivered by boat this morning?' she asked, as she watched him spread the selection of papers out for her perusal.

'Yes, *mademoiselle*. No matter where we are in the world,

Monsieur Lombardi likes his papers delivered out to the yacht.'

Of course, Isobel thought wryly—everyone should have the morning post and papers delivered direct to their yacht. She smiled as she flicked her eye over them, deciding that this was a piece of information she would definitely include in her article. The papers were mostly in French and Italian, but she noticed a couple of English ones amongst the mix. They were all financial papers—no *Daily Banner,* of course.

She took a sip of her coffee before returning her attention to the boxes. There was a letter attached to the top one, and with a jolt of surprise she saw it had her name on it.

Quickly she slit the envelope open, and pulled out the crisp sheet of white paper.

Izzy, hope you slept well. Meet me for lunch at the flower market in Nice. Restaurant Chez Henri, one o'clock, and don't be late, Marco.

It was more of a summons than an invitation, Isobel thought as her eyes flicked over the bold, clear handwriting.

Hope you slept well, indeed! And how could she meet him for lunch when she had no clothes? Unless…

She looked at the boxes underneath, and quickly unloosened the red ribbon and lifted the first lid.

Nestled in amongst folds of tissue lay a silk dress in the most exquisite shades of green and purple. Even before she looked at the label she knew it was an expensive designer dress. It was in her size too!

She opened the next box and found a pair of gold Jimmy Choo high-heeled shoes with a matching clutch bag.

Isobel swallowed hard. Never in her entire life had she owned an outfit so beautiful or so expensive.

But somehow it didn't seem right, accepting such gifts from

a man she had just slept with. She felt a bit like a mistress or a kept woman or something.

With a frown, she put the lid back on the boxes.

She had to think sensibly. If she didn't accept the clothes she wouldn't be able to meet Marco for lunch. And maybe… just maybe…he would give her an interview today. Then she'd be able to put this episode behind her, go back to London and forget all about Marco Lombardi.

At exactly twelve-forty-five Isobel was skimming across the sea in a speedboat that was taking her from Marco's yacht into Nice Harbour.

As the boat slowed and entered the port she smoothed back her hair with a feeling of apprehension. She hoped she was going to be able to deal with this lunch in a purely professional way—that she could look at Marco and forget what had happened between them.

The boat pulled alongside the quay and a man in the same uniform as the man who was piloting her came hurrying to help her step out onto dry land.

Marco seemed to have a lot of staff; whilst she'd been lazing aboard his yacht this morning she'd counted at least five people wearing that uniform.

There was a limousine waiting for her next to the dock. And Isobel was aware of a few curious glances being thrown her way as a chauffeur got out to open the passenger door for her.

She wasn't used to so much attention, and she had to admit she felt good; the dress she was wearing was fabulous. It was perfectly cut, skimming over her curves in a very flattering way, and it even had short, feathery little straps that covered the bruise on her shoulder. It seemed Marco had thought of everything. All she lacked was some make-up—not that her appearance was important, she reminded herself firmly. Really she should be focusing on work.

Isobel looked out of the limousine with interest as they drove around the quayside. She loved the colourful buildings and the quaint old-world charm about the place. They passed pavement cafés and restaurants, and then swept past a huge memorial to the fallen of World Wars. Further around the headland she could see the Bay of Angels glittering in the sun, and the long sweep of the Promenade des Anglais.

The limousine turned off the main road at that point, through an archway into what looked like an old medieval part of the town, before pulling to a stop.

'Monsieur Lombardi is waiting for you,' the chauffeur told her as he opened the door for her and pointed towards a cobbled street lined with pavement restaurants.

She felt a bit like a nervous teenager on a first date as she walked in the direction the chauffeur had indicated. With determination, she held her head up high. This was just a business lunch, she told herself over and over again. It would be madness to think of it in any other way. She tried to concentrate on the beauty of her surroundings, the lovely old buildings in rich shades of yellow and umber, the profusion of flowers on the stalls in the centre of the street, the scent of carnations and lilies and roses merging in the warmth of the day with the French buzz of the market.

She saw Marco before he saw her. He was sitting at one of the pavement cafés, studying the menu, and he looked so relaxed and sophisticated in his dark suit and white shirt that she felt all her sensible thoughts immediately start to desert her.

Was this gorgeous man really waiting for her? she wondered dreamily. Had last night really happened, or had it been some kind of crazy hallucination? None of this felt real, somehow.

He looked up, and her senses flipped even more as she saw the look of surprise in his eyes as he took in her appearance. 'Izzy, you look great,' he said as he got to his feet.

'Thank you.' She felt suddenly unbearably self-conscious. She wished she was wearing make-up—she wished that she were as beautiful as the women he usually dated. A dart of anger rushed through her at the absurdity of that thought.

This wasn't a real date, she reminded herself firmly. And even if it were, she knew what type of man he was—knew that even if she were the most beautiful woman in the world, his interest in her would probably go no deeper than last night's sex. And he'd most likely even forgotten *that*.

'The dress suits you.' He took his seat again as she sat down.

'Yes…thank you. I take it you have a secretary who is good at shopping in her coffee break?'

He laughed. 'Actually, I saw it in a boutique window as I walked up to the office. But you are right—I have a very obliging secretary who ran out for it in her coffee break.'

And was probably used to doing such things, Isobel reminded herself matter-of-factly. 'Well, thanks anyway. I was a bit unsure about accepting it, but I thought arriving for lunch wearing a dressing gown might cause a bit of a stir.'

'I'm sure it would have done. Because you looked very sexy in that as well,' he told her with a gleam in his eye.

Maybe he hadn't forgotten last night.

She tried desperately not to look in any way uncomfortable about the remark, but she could feel herself heating up as she remembered how he had untied that robe last night—how he had moved his hands boldly over her naked body.

'So, how are you today?' he asked nonchalantly as he put up a hand to summon the waiter.

'Absolutely fine.' Isobel forced herself to hold her head high and maintain eye contact. She could do this, she told herself firmly. She could be just as casual as he—could forget all about what had happened between them.

'Good.' His gaze moved slowly over her. He'd thought that she would look good with her hair down and the right clothes, but he hadn't realised she would be this striking. Her long dark hair lay in glossy curls around her shoulders, and although she wasn't wearing any make-up her skin was smoothly perfect and her lips had a natural apricot glow. She really was naturally stunning, he thought absently.

But it was her eyes that held him—she looked so determined and yet at the same time so…defenceless. The combination intrigued him, made him remember how sweetly and innocently she had responded to him in bed.

'I enjoyed last night,' he told her lazily.

He watched with interest as the skin over her high cheekbones seemed to flare with a wild rose colour. He couldn't remember the last time he'd made a woman blush like that.

'Yes…it was…OK.' It took every ounce of Isobel's self-control to make the nonchalant reply. What she really wanted to do was to get up from the table and run as far away as she possibly could. She couldn't handle this. She was mortified… absolutely mortified.

He laughed. 'Yes, it was definitely OK,' he told her, and the husky, teasing warmth in his tone made her skin flush even more.

She looked over at him from beneath the long dark sweep of her eyelashes and he smiled. Yesterday he had wondered if that shy look was for real…now he knew that it was.

And she was obviously struggling to cope with this situation.

'So, how was your business meeting this morning?' She tried to change the subject.

'To be honest, it was an extreme inconvenience,' he told her softly.

'Was it…?' From nowhere she suddenly remembered how at one point last night she'd sleepily suggested that he forgot about business today.

'Absolutely.' His lips twisted in a half-smile. 'Another few hours in bed would have been most welcome.'

'Marco, I think you should know that I wasn't thinking very clearly last night...or this morning, for that matter.' She cut across him breathlessly. 'So if you don't mind I'd rather we didn't spend time analysing what happened.'

He smiled. 'Isobel, I kind of gathered that. Neither of us planned for last night. It was one of those things—chemistry, Karma...call it what you want.'

She nodded, and tried to tell herself that she was glad they'd had that conversation and cleared the air. Except as she looked over at him things didn't feel any less complicated.

'Now, shall we order some lunch?' he suggested matter-of-factly as the waiter stopped beside their table.

'Yes, of course.' She grabbed the menu and tried to study it. But she wasn't in any way interested in anything that was on it, and she was so wound up she didn't think she could eat anything.

'The seafood is good here,' Marco told her. 'Also the Salade Niçoise is a speciality of the region.'

Isobel grabbed on to the suggestion gratefully. 'I'll have the salad, then, thank you.'

Marco nodded and gave the order in perfect French.

She tried not to think about how sexy he sounded—tried not to think about anything connected with last night. But as he turned his attention lazily back to her she could feel herself heating up even more.

He seemed so perfectly at ease. But then she supposed he was used to going to bed with a woman without thinking deeply about it.

By contrast, as she looked at his hands all she could remember was the way he had caressed her. When she looked at his lips she was remembering the way they had possessed hers. And as their eyes held across the table she wanted him all over again.

The knowledge twisted painfully inside her. So much for hoping he was out of her system! So much for being able to act as if last night had never happened! Her reassurances to herself about getting with the modern programme now felt hollow and foolish—like a very bad joke.

She didn't want to feel like this.

Marco's gaze drifted over her, taking in the vulnerable gleam in her eyes, the pallor of her skin. The chemistry was still swirling between them, and he knew he only had to reach for her to break down the flimsy defences that she was so desperate to construct around herself.

He was tempted to do that right now—because for the last few hours of his business meetings he had been distractedly thinking about possessing her body again.

But something in her eyes held him back, told him to bide his time, take this slowly.

She was his for the taking…but he found himself in the unusual position of wanting to take things at a leisurely pace—of wanting to explore her mind as well as her body. He was interested by the fact that he had taken her virginity—fascinated about why even now she was so scared of letting go and opening up to him.

Most women fell over themselves for so much as a smile from him…but she was different.

OK, since his divorce he hadn't wanted to get involved with any woman, especially a journalist, but he did have a little time on his hands before he took a business flight to New York in a few days, and she was…very appealing.

'Actually, I have some news for you. My deal with Cheri Bon was finalised this morning,' he told her.

'Really?' She sat up a little straighter. 'Are you going to tell me all about it?'

He smiled at her. 'I just might.'

For now he'd play along with her need to be businesslike—but after lunch things were going to change, he told himself determinedly.

CHAPTER EIGHT

THE sun was warm on Isobel's back. The food was good and the conversation stimulating. Marco was giving her the inside details of his takeover deal with the French confectionery company, and it was completely absorbing.

'When you make up your mind that you want something, you really go for it, don't you?' she murmured with a shake of her head.

'Don't you?' He looked at her humorously. 'Aren't you the young woman who hung around the Sienna offices for weeks to get the inside track on what was happening there?'

'I was convinced you were about to take the place apart...' She looked over at him guiltily. 'Sorry—but there was a factory last year in London that you *did* close.'

'Henshaws...' Marco shook his head. 'That company was dead in the water when I bought it, Izzy. It was the land that was valuable.'

'Yeah, well, I thought it was similar to what had happened at my grandfather's firm...and, yes, I realise I got it wrong.'

He shook his head and watched as she looked away from him. 'It still hurts you to think about what happened with your family's firm, doesn't it?'

She shrugged self-consciously. 'I just feel like an idiot for being shocked. I honestly didn't think my dad could hurt me any more than he had...'

Marco's dark eyes moved over her slowly.

'Anyway, let's not talk about that,' she said hurriedly.

'No, let's not. Have I told you that you are the first reporter that I've actually wanted to spend time with?' He leaned forward and reached to tuck a stray strand of her hair behind her ear. 'It's very curious,' he murmured huskily.

The words and the touch of his hand made her emotions flip.

She wanted to tell him that she liked spending time with him too. But she forced herself not to because that would be madness…emotional suicide. He was a player, she told herself for the hundredth time…and he was playing her right now.

His phone rang and he reached lazily to answer it, his eyes still on her face.

He was speaking in Italian now. She remembered how he'd spoken to her in Italian last night, and how she'd asked him to translate words in between kisses. The memory sent little butterflies dancing around in her stomach. They hadn't been loving words, they had been sexy, tantalising…provoking words, and just thinking about them made her feel hot all over again.

Frantically she tried to bury the memory—it didn't help.

Marco hung up and put his phone back on the table. 'Unfortunately I'm going to have to call by the office before we head back to the yacht. You don't mind, do you?'

'No, of course not.' The thought of going back to the yacht with him made her very apprehensive anyway. It was all very well keeping up a pretence here, while they were surrounded by people, but once they were alone…how would she deal with her feelings for him then?

'You know, I do believe there is a storm coming in,' he observed suddenly as he summoned the waiter to ask for the bill.

Isobel hadn't even noticed the weather until he'd pointed it out, but now that she looked around she saw dark clouds were sweeping in from the direction of the sea.

They left the table, and Marco reached to take hold of her arm as they walked through the square and then turned up a narrow side street.

Isobel told herself she should pull away from him, but somehow she couldn't make herself. There was something enchanting about strolling along beside him through the atmospheric streets. It was a little like stepping back in time, the houses were so old and picturesque, and some had windowsills packed with bright flowerboxes or canaries in cages.

'Is this your first time in Nice?' Marco asked as he noticed how she was taking in the surroundings.

'Yes…I've never been to the South of France before.'

'Really? Well, if we get some time I'll have to show you around.'

'That would be fun…' She glanced up at him, not sure if that was a serious offer or not. 'Although I'm not supposed to be on holiday.'

'Me neither.' He smiled. 'But we could play hooky a little.'

The teasing suggestion sounded good, but before she got a chance to answer it started to rain. Huge fat drops splattered down—slowly at first.

'Come on—we'd better hurry.' Marco's hand tightened on her arm as he picked up the pace.

The afternoon was growing strangely dark, and a low growl of thunder tore through the air, reverberating through the narrow streets.

People were scattering for cover now, and the rain suddenly started to lash with torrential force—as if someone was tipping buckets down from the heavens.

One moment Isobel was a little wet, and the next she was soaked.

Marco pulled her into the shelter of the first doorway. There wasn't much room, and they huddled closely under the small awning, watching the rain bounce and people running.

'Wow! What's happened to the day?' she laughed.

'When it rains here it really rains—that's why the countryside is so lush and green.' Marco turned his attention from the weather to her, his dark eyes moving over her in concern. 'Are you OK?'

'I'm fine.'

He brushed a wet strand of hair back from her face. 'You're completely soaked.'

'So are you.' For a moment all she could do was look up at him. And suddenly the rain was forgotten as she noticed how his gaze had moved to her lips.

She wanted him to kiss her, she realised...wanted it so much...

As he lowered his head and his mouth captured hers she surrendered immediately to the warmth of his lips, kissing him back hungrily.

Marco released her after a few moments. 'It's a long time since I kissed someone in a shop doorway,' he said with a grin.

'Yes, me too. I think I was sixteen.'

'I think I would have liked to know you at sixteen,' he said teasingly. 'However, I think the age difference might have been a bit much back then.'

For some reason Isobel wished she'd known him at sixteen too...and that she had been a different sixteen-year-old—one who could have been carefree...one who could have kissed him and had time to while away an afternoon without care instead of rushing to get home, frightened by what she might find...

He looked past her. 'The rain seems to be abating. Shall we make a dash for my office? It's not far from here.'

She nodded. 'I can't get much wetter anyway.'

As they stepped back out into the street Isobel tried not to analyse what was happening between them. It felt too real... too good. She'd spent her life trying to be sensible and careful, trying to avoid heartbreak, and where had it got her? she asked herself fiercely.

Marco cut across to another road.

They were at the back of a large building now, which had electric gates. Marco tapped in a security code on the brass box on the post, and the gates swung open into lush gardens.

'Welcome to the Lombardi headquarters.'

The old mansion house was painted yellow, its white shutters thrown open to the day.

'I didn't expect an office to be quite this beautiful,' Isobel said in surprise.

'It was my mother's home when she was a child. It dates from the early nineteenth century.'

'What a shame to have turned it into offices.'

'I know, but it's conveniently located, and as I'm usually short of time, that's what counts these days.'

Marco led her into a grand entrance hall with a sweeping staircase. At one side there were doors leading through to the offices. The building had obviously been very sympathetically converted, so as not to take away from the natural beauty of the place, and from the glimpse Isobel had the results seemed to have led to a very pleasant working environment.

A secretary came hurrying out with a pile of post in her arms and spoke to Marco in French. Isobel wondered if she was the one who had been sent out to buy her dress. She was blonde and probably about eighteen or nineteen, wearing a black T-shirt and mini skirt with ankle boots.

She was very attractive, and Isobel couldn't help noticing how she smiled at Marco before she handed him the post and headed back to her office. Probably half his workforce was in love with him, Isobel thought idly. Even with his dark hair wet and slicked back from his face he looked too damn handsome.

'Right, Isobel, we may as well go and try to dry off and

have some coffee upstairs,' Marco said as he led the way towards a lift. 'I'll phone the chauffeur to come pick us up.'

Isobel thought that when they stepped from the elevator upstairs they were just going to be in another office, but when the doors slid back on the top floor she found herself in a very elegant apartment, with tiled black and white floors.

'This is lovely,' she murmured as Marco showed her through to the drawing room.

'Yes, I had the interior decoration done by someone who is an expert on the period. They've restored it almost exactly as it would have looked when it was first built.'

'It's very stylish.' She ran her hand over a piece of antique French furniture that looked as if it was worth a small fortune, then moved to the doors that led to the balcony. On a good day the view over the Mediterranean was probably spectacular, but today the sea was almost obliterated by dark clouds and lashing rain.

As Isobel looked out a vivid gash of lightning lit the sky.

'This storm doesn't seem to be going away,' she murmured. 'I'm almost glad we're not back on the yacht.'

'You would be perfectly safe out there. In fact it's very exhilarating to be out at sea in an electrical storm.' Marco had been flicking through his post, but as he glanced up the outline of her body distracted him. The damp dress was clinging very provocatively to her curves, highlighting just how fabulous her figure really was.

And as she turned to look at him he realised he wanted her right here...*right now.*

'But we don't need to go back to the yacht tonight. We can just stay here,' he told her huskily.

Isobel knew exactly what he was saying to her. There was no mistaking his tone, or the sudden predatory gleam in the darkness of his gaze as he looked at her.

The really scary thing was that she felt an answering

surge of need straight away, and she didn't want to fight it any more.

'That sounds…like a plan,' she murmured, her heart suddenly starting to thunder against her chest as he moved closer.

Her eyes were wide and jewel-bright as she looked up at him. How had he ever thought for one moment that she was plain? Marco wondered. How had he not noticed how lovely her bone structure was, how soft and inviting her lips were?

And as for her body… His eyes raked down over the firm thrust of her breasts against the silk fabric. Just looking at her made him grow hard with desire.

'You know, you looked great in this outfit over lunch, *cara*…' he murmured. 'But I have to say I like the wet look even better.' As he spoke he smoothed the straps of her dress down and bent to kiss her shoulder. At the same time he ran his fingertips over the wet silk, caressing the hard thrust of her nipples. 'In fact I think you should dress like this all the time.'

Isobel discovered she was so turned on she couldn't find her breath to answer him.

'I like being able to see the gorgeous thrust of your nipples…the pert shape of your *derrière*.'

'Marco!' She blushed fiercely, and he laughed as he gently tugged the silky material down a little further and kissed the exposed creamy curve of her breast.

'Have I told you how much I like that librarian-type streak you have?' he asked throatily.

'You mean…used to have…' she murmured unsteadily, and then gasped with pleasure as his head moved lower and his mouth found her nipple, the warmth of his tongue licking over her, tormenting her with wild pleasure.

There was a loud roar of thunder outside, and it seemed to echo the feelings that were blazing through her entire body.

She moaned softly, desire eating her away, and then his lips were on hers, silencing her, dominating her senses, until she felt she would go out of her mind if she didn't get closer.

'I want you right now, Izzy,' he breathed. 'I want to possess your body over and over again...until I'm completely sated.'

The words were a command, and they made her temperature soar. She wanted him right now as well. Her body was demanding fulfilment with an urgency that was taking her over, leaving no room for embarrassment or shame or any kind of rational thought.

He kissed her with a fire that seemed to sizzle through her entire body, and then he lifted her up to place her onto the table, sweeping the letters and packages there onto the floor with complete impatience.

He pushed up her dress, his fingers stroking up along the naked length of her thighs, and then roughly pulled at her panties, tearing the flimsy silk away from her.

She pressed herself closer, her legs wrapped around him. Then shuddered with pleasure as she felt the hardness of his body against the warm, sweet sensitive core of her.

'Where has my shy, sweet librarian-type gone now?' he teased. 'Come—let me hear how much you want me.'

'Don't torment me, Marco...' she replied, running her hands up over his shirt, trying to unbutton it and failing miserably because she was so impatient for him. 'You know I want you.'

He reached and unzipped her dress. It fell down, leaving her completely naked from the waist up. 'But I find I *want* to torment you, *cara*,' he murmured. 'I want to hear how much you want me.'

He said something in Italian...something that sounded hot and steamy and made her senses pound. Then his lips moved to nuzzle against her breast.

'I ache for you...' She closed her eyes on a wave of ecstasy.

'And I thought you just wanted to forget all of this and

be practical...' He looked up at her and watched how she blushed.

'I do... I mean, I did... But not now...'

He laughed.

'Marco, I...need you...right now...please!' Her eyes opened and met with his and he smiled. He knew he could make her beg for him...knew that all her sensible words over lunch meant nothing, that this chemistry between them was a long way from being over.

'Patience...*cara*.' He reached for some condoms that he had placed in his jacket pocket earlier. 'I need to put some protection on...'

'I don't want to be patient!' She sat further up. Her hair had started to dry and it looked glossy and gypsy-like, and her eyes were wide with need as they met with his.

He had never seen her look more beautiful than she did in that moment, and he felt his stomach clenching as he fought to keep control.

She slid slightly back and then boldly brought her hand down to stroke him. She wanted to be in control for a little while, she thought fiercely, and she wanted him now.

She saw the flare of heat in the darkness of his eyes, and then he kissed her lips hungrily and suddenly other forces took over. It was as if a wildfire had swiftly broken through the flimsy barriers they had tried to set up, and now it raged out of control, consuming them both totally. Neither of them was in control any more. Neither of them could think clearly any more. All they could do was fiercely try to get closer to each other, to devour each other, to try somehow to quench the flames burning so urgently inside them.

Contraception was completely forgotten. And when release finally gripped Isobel it was so pleasurable that she found herself almost dizzy with the wild sensations.

At that point it took every ounce of Marco's restraint to

try and pull back. They clung to each other breathlessly, and it took a while for any reality to return.

Her head was pressed close against Marco's chest and his arms were tightly around her. She could hear the heavy beat of his heart and it seemed to echo her own—as if their bodies were still in unison for those seconds. A clock chimed somewhere, the melodic silvery tones resounding through the emptiness of the apartment and merging with the heaviness of their breathing.

'What just happened?' She was the first to speak, her voice shaky with incredulity, and he found himself laughing, his hand moving to stroke tenderly over her dark silky hair.

'I think the South of France was just rocked by a major earthquake.'

She smiled sleepily; she didn't understand why she was behaving so wildly, so rashly. All she knew was that she liked being held like this and she didn't want to move away from him—because when she did she knew that she would start to question herself, and she didn't want to think that deeply right now. 'Well, I think we just about survived.'

'Just about,' he agreed lazily.

He'd never lost control like that before in his life—was always so careful about using contraception. It was as if a mist had come down over him and he'd only just managed to draw back at the very last moment after sating her.

He hoped it was enough.

It *had* to be enough he told himself, angry with himself.

'Marco, are you OK?' she murmured suddenly as the hazy mists of pleasure started to lift and she realised he was looking at her with a different blaze in his eyes now.

'We were playing with fire, *cara*…'

Isobel knew what he was talking about straight away—and that was amazing, because up until that minute she hadn't even stopped to think about it.

He saw the realisation dawning in her eyes, saw the sudden fear there. 'Marco, what on earth was I thinking?'

The panic-stricken question almost made him smile.

'Probably the same as me—only about pleasure.'

Her skin flared with heat. It seemed there was no limit to her stupidity around him. Horrified, she drew away from him and started to pull up her dress, cover herself up.

'Hey!' He put a hand under her chin before she could pull away from him. 'What just happened between us was incredible…and neither of us were thinking particularly clearly. Don't beat yourself up about this, *cara*…we are in it together.'

The gentle words and the touch of his hand made her want to melt back into his arms.

'Besides, I did manage to exercise restraint, so it's probably fine.' He pulled her closer and kissed her.

And when he released her her heart was beating in a different mode. There was something about the way he touched her that could turn her on so quickly…

She looked away from him hurriedly, not wanting him to know how he was affecting her—again!

'Maybe I should go and have a shower, or a bath or something.'

He smiled. 'Make yourself at home. The bathroom is down the hall to the right,' he told her easily, and watched as she smoothed down her dress before she slid from the table.

He should have taken more care of her, he told himself angrily as he watched her walk away from him. The door closed behind her and he moved to the window to look out.

What the hell had he been thinking? He'd been so careful since his divorce to keep an emotional distance from the women he dated. He didn't want to get involved with *anyone* on a deep level.

Which made the risk he had just taken with Isobel totally unacceptable!

It was still raining outside—hard, unforgiving rain that bounced and hissed against the tiles on the patio.

For a second he found himself remembering a day in California when the weather had been exactly like this. The day Lucinda had lost their baby.

He swept a hand through his hair as he tried to block the memory out. They had wanted their child so much, and he had never felt so helpless...so wretched.

But it was done...it was over. Lucy was getting on with her life putting it behind her, and he was doing the same. For him life now revolved around work, with the occasional casual interlude with a woman—and that was all he wanted.

He turned away from the window and noticed the letters he had swept onto the floor earlier. He found himself remembering how much he had wanted Isobel...how fiercely he had needed her.

He frowned and went to pick the envelopes up.

She was a journalist, he reminded himself tersely, so it was never going to be more than a casual fling.

OK, there was something different about her and even thinking about her now made him want her again. But some women just took a little longer to get out of the system, he told himself swiftly. That was all it was.

CHAPTER NINE

ISOBEL tore the dress from over her head and stepped under the pounding jet of the shower. Was it only this morning that she had sworn to herself that this wasn't going to happen again? What was wrong with her? Why was she being so weak?

She raised her head to the jet of water and allowed it to pummel down over her face as she tried to clear her mind. But nothing made sense—certainly not the fact that she hadn't even thought about something as vital as contraception. The very thought made her temperature rise with panic.

How had she gone from being so sensible and so determined not to make a mistake to the other side of the scale so quickly?

Marco was completely wrong for her...the antithesis, in fact, of everything she'd told herself she wanted in a man. She knew the relationship wasn't going anywhere—knew that when she flew home to London she wouldn't see him again.

And yet when he touched her, when he looked at her in that certain way, none of that seemed to matter. She still wanted him.

She got out of the shower and wrapped herself in one of the large fluffy towels. There was a hairdryer next to the dressing table unit and she gave her hair a quick blast with it, teasing her fingers through the long dark strands until it dried into glossy curls.

It was a few moments before she realised she wasn't alone.

Marco was standing behind her, leaning indolently against the open doorway, watching her.

She flicked the hairdryer off and their eyes met in the mirror.

'I made you a coffee.' He came in and put the china mug down on the countertop.

'Thanks.' Her heart started to pound as, instead of leaving, he leaned against the wall beside her. She noticed he'd changed out of his suit and was wearing jeans and a white T-shirt. She'd never seen him dressed so casually, and the look suited him.

'My clothes were a bit rain-washed,' he said as he saw her looking at him.

'Yes, my dress is the same.'

'You look good in the towel,' he said huskily.

She tried not to feel self-conscious as his gaze drifted down over her—after all, he'd seen her without any clothes, so being wrapped in a towel was an improvement in the modesty stakes. However, she still felt shy, and the situation felt far too intimate.

'Is it still raining out there?' she asked—more for something to say than anything else.

'Yes, it is… What is it you English say…? Throwing it down in cats?'

'Raining cats and dogs,' she corrected him, and smiled. Most of the time his English was absolutely perfect, but he sounded so…so *sexy* when he got it slightly wrong.

She put her coffee down again and tried not to think too deeply about that.

'So I gave the chauffeur the night off,' he said quietly. 'I thought we might as well stay here.'

Her heart seemed to do a crazy skip, and she tried very hard to ignore it and be sensible. 'Marco, do you think that's a good idea…? I mean, maybe we should be getting back to reality.'

'Maybe we should,' he agreed lazily.

'I should be focusing on my article and—'

'And you keep getting distracted,' he finished for her with a smile.

'Yes.'

'If it makes you feel any better I have a pile of paperwork I should be doing, and I feel equally distracted.' His glance moved to her curves, so provocatively concealed under the white fluffy towel.

'It doesn't make me feel that much better,' she whispered hoarsely.

'Well, let's see if I *can* make you feel better.' Marco reached and traced a playful finger over the edge of the towel. 'We will just have to make time count now…'

He didn't even wait for her to answer—just tugged at the material so that it loosened and fell to the floor.

One more night wouldn't hurt, he told himself as he reached to pull her into his arms.

When Isobel woke she was lying in Marco's large double bed, cradled in his arms. She loved being here with him like this, she thought drowsily, loved the feeling of her body held close against his powerful physique.

Somewhere outside church bells were ringing, and daylight was slanting in through a chink in the curtains.

She turned her head slightly and glanced up at him. His eyes were closed and his handsome features were relaxed, but she wasn't sure if he was asleep or not. For a little while she allowed herself to drink him in, her gaze resting on the sensual line of his lips, the square jaw, the dark thickness of his hair. No man had a right to be so good-looking or so good in bed, she thought hazily.

Last night had been incredible.

She wanted to reach up and trace her fingers over the smooth olive tones of his skin. But if she did she would probably wake him up—and if she woke him up he would discover that the sky outside the bedroom window had turned an oyster-pink and the sun was slowly starting to rise over the city.

And once he discovered that, their time together in this apartment would be over. He'd probably want to get back to work. She remembered last night he'd said he had a pile of paperwork waiting for him. Maybe he would even throw a few facts at her for her article and have her packed off back to London by nightfall.

She frowned, cross with herself for feeling down about it. She should be keen to get her interview and leave, and she shouldn't for one moment expect anything more. Because, according to the newspapers, since his divorce his relationships had lasted no more than two days max. And this was no relationship… She wasn't even his type… She didn't know what this was. She supposed her old sensible self would say it was some kind of madness…and she'd probably be right. But right now Isobel didn't want to acknowledge that.

Marco opened his eyes suddenly and caught her watching him. She blushed.

'Morning, sleepyhead.'

'Actually, I think you are the sleepy one. I've been awake for ages,' she retorted, trying to sound as if she was totally indifferent about waking up with him. 'I just didn't want to disturb you by disentangling myself.'

'Is that right?' He didn't sound in the slightest bit fooled. 'So how come you were snoring ten minutes ago?'

'I was not!' She looked at him in consternation. 'For one thing, I don't snore!'

'How do you know if you haven't slept with anyone before?' He laughed as he rolled her over so that he was pinning her to the bed.

His hands were linked through hers, holding them back

against the pillows behind her head. She wriggled a little to get free, but he didn't release her.

For a moment he just looked at her, hardly able to believe how beautiful she was with her hair spread out around her on the pillows, her skin all flushed from his teasing, her lips slightly pouted. She really didn't look like the same woman who had stormed into his office in her starchy buttoned-up blouse, that was for sure.

He frowned. 'And how come you *haven't* slept with anyone before?' he asked softly. 'When you are so...deliciously good at it?'

The husky question made her deeply uncomfortable. She really didn't want to discuss her sex-life—or lack of it—with him. 'Let's not waste time on my past, Marco.'

'Why not?' One dark eyebrow rose.

'Because I told you I'm not that interesting.' She tried to look away from him, but he nibbled on the side of her neck, making her laugh breathlessly, making her look back at him.

'Now, come on... As I introduced you to the sport in question, why don't you humour me with the truth?'

'A sport...? Is that how you see it?' She looked into his eyes and saw a flicker of emotion there that she couldn't quite work out.

'Well, maybe since my divorce I haven't taken it as seriously as I should...' His dark eyes moved over her solemnly for a moment.

The husky admission made her still. 'Because you've been so cut up?'

He hesitated. '*Sì*... Cut up, as you put it...' He added something else in Italian, and she would have given anything to be able to understand him.

'Marco, I don't know what you are saying.'

For a second he hesitated, and she wondered if he was

going to explain further, but then the expression in his eyes became veiled.

'Good, because what I said was not important,' he told her lightly.

She didn't believe him—because she had understood the bleak look she had glimpsed for just a moment. She wondered if he would have opened up more to her if she wasn't a journalist.

The thought made her frown. 'Marco, I—'

'Hey, what is important right at this moment is you...' He cut across her gently and released her hands to trail one finger slowly over the little frown marks between her eyes, smoothing them away and sending little shivers of desire through her. 'I don't think it is any secret that I enjoy making love—that I think it is one of life's great pleasures.'

The words made the shivers of need inside her escalate.

'But I was asking about you...and how you see things,' he finished firmly.

She wanted to be so much closer to him... She felt a dart of anger at herself for wanting it so much...for wanting to get inside his skin and know exactly what he was feeling.

If she did she might not like what she saw, she reminded herself fiercely. He was a master of evasiveness and a heartbreaker. And yet... There was something about him that made her just want to trust him. And she was starting to think that he wasn't as cavalier about his marriage break-up as she had first believed.

'Izzy, we are talking about *you*,' he reminded her firmly.

'Believe me, Marco, there is nothing mystical about my lack of experience. I just never got around to that...particular sport.' She hoped he would leave it like that.

But he was continuing to look at her, as if fascinated by her reply.

'It was just circumstances,' she whispered helplessly. 'My

mother was ill for a long time after her marriage broke up, and she went through a series of disastrous relationships...'

For a moment she was quiet as she remembered all the times she had hurried home from school, worried about what she would find.

'And someone had to be the sensible one...hmm?'

She shrugged. 'As soon as I was old enough I got a job in the evenings to try and support my studies—as I said, it was just circumstances.'

'But then you met someone and got engaged?'

'Yes...big mistake.' As he released his hold on her she managed to slide away from under him. 'Rob just caught me at a point in my life when I was feeling lonely. It was never a passionate relationship. In fact I think I thought of him more as a friend than anything else, and I was busy building my career.'

She sat with her back to him at the edge of the bed. 'When he suggested we get married and said that he was OK about waiting to consummate our relationship until our wedding night it sounded...romantic.' She bit down on the softness of her lip. 'Anyway, to cut a long story short, I called round to his apartment one night and found him otherwise occupied with another woman. We'd only been engaged a week.' She flicked a look over her shoulder at Marco. 'Silly me.'

'The guy sounds like an idiot,' Marco said brusquely.

She smiled. 'Thanks, but I think I was the idiot for agreeing to marry him.'

Marco's shirt was hanging over the side of the chair beside the bed, and she reached to put it on rather than walk naked across the bedroom. 'You know, we should be talking about you...not me,' she told him as she pulled it across her body and turned to look at him.

'We should... But despite what you say you are so much more interesting—especially dressed in my shirt.' There was a gleam in his eye that made her senses quicken.

Hastily she moved away from the bed, trying to think sensibly. 'You could get a degree in being evasive, you know.'

'Could I, indeed?' He leaned back against the pillows and watched as she walked around the end of the bed to draw the curtains back, admiring the long length of her legs, the sway of her hips.

'How's the day looking?' he asked.

She stood for a moment, admiring the view. 'It's perfect,' she murmured, gazing out over the red roofs and the clear blue sky towards the glitter of the sea. 'It's as if the storm has washed everything clean and it's all shiny and new.'

She turned to look at him, noticing the way he was watching her.

He was so vital, so extremely masculine and attractive, that it was difficult to drag her eyes away from him—but she did.

'Right, I'm going to see if my dress is dry. Do you want a coffee or something while I'm in the kitchen?' She headed to move past him out of the door, but he reached and caught hold of her arm and drew her back onto the bed beside him with ease.

'What I want is an early-morning kiss...' he murmured huskily as his lips claimed hers.

She kissed him back. She couldn't help herself. It just felt so wonderful.

'That's better...' He released her, and for a moment they just stared into each other's eyes. 'Now, I suggest you get dressed and then I'll take you out for breakfast and we'll make the most of this brand-new day together...hmm?'

She nodded. 'I'd like that, Marco,' she said softly.

When Marco had suggested breakfast she'd thought they would just wander through the city streets and find a pavement café, but instead when they stepped outside there was a shiny red convertible sports car waiting for them on the drive.

'Wow...this is a fabulous car,' she murmured as he opened the passenger door for her and she settled herself into the luxurious leather interior. 'I didn't see this when we arrived yesterday. How has it just appeared as if by magic outside your front door?'

Marco laughed as he went around to the driving seat. 'Sorry, *cara*, there is no magic involved, I just phoned down and asked a member of staff to take it out of the garage for me.'

'I'm still pretty impressed. Everything seems to run so smoothly and effortlessly around you.'

'Not always, Izzy...believe me, not always.' He found a pair of sunglasses on the dashboard and put them on. Then he flicked the ignition switch and the powerful car flared into life with a low, throaty growl.

It was a good feeling, driving down the Promenade des Anglais beside Marco. It was still early, but already the sun was beating down with some power, and the warm breeze that drifted in over them was deliciously refreshing.

She admired the scenery, and Marco told her a little of the town's history. He pointed out the Hotel Negresco, with its impressive Belle Époque architecture—probably one of the most elite of hotels, built with only the rich and famous in mind.

As they stopped at traffic lights Isobel noticed how women glanced over at Marco. The Italian car and the Italian driver were a head-turning combination, she thought wryly. Yet Marco seemed totally unaware of the interest.

'I thought we should take breakfast along one of the most scenic coastal roads in the world, the Corniche d'Or, and then head out to St Tropez.'

'Sounds great,' Isobel said happily. 'What time have you got to be back?'

He laughed at that. 'Izzy, I don't have to be back at all,'

he said with a shake of his head. 'There is no point being the boss if you can't take a day off when you want.'

She glanced over at him in surprise. 'Oh, right—I just thought you had lots of paperwork to do.'

'I have, but it can wait. Finalising the deal yesterday with Cheri Bon has freed me up a bit.' Marco found himself lying. He was supposed to be in a meeting this morning with his board of directors, but he'd rung to postpone it when Isobel had been taking her shower.

He still couldn't work out why. It was a long time since he'd put work on the back burner in order to spend time with a woman. But it was just a one-off, he told himself firmly. He deserved a day playing tourist—he'd been working too hard recently. And Izzy was remarkably good company...*for a journalist*. And good on the eye too, he thought, his gaze flicking over her curvaceous body. That dress looked great on her...although he had to admit he still preferred the wet look.

He shifted up a gear as they headed out of town. 'I think I'll ring and get the yacht to pick us up from somewhere around Cannes. We could sail the rest of the way down to St Tropez, or go over to the Îles de Lérins, if you'd prefer?'

'I'm happy to place myself in your hands...' She flushed as she realised what she had just said. 'If you know what I mean.'

'Yes, I know what you mean.' He smiled. 'And that's fine with me, *cara*,' he assured her softly. 'Let's just enjoy the day...hmm?'

It was amazing how one minute she could feel tense around him and the next blissfully relaxed. It was like being on some kind of rollercoaster. Best just not to think too deeply and go with the flow, she told herself as she looked out at the spectacular views.

They drove along the highway out of Nice, and through some little villages until they reached Cannes, with its glitzy hotels and palm-lined promenade. There were giant placards up everywhere, advertising the film festival, and Isobel read them with interest, recognising famous names with excitement. 'I forgot the Film Festival was on, I suppose the place will be awash with famous stars right now?'

'Yes, it will be pretty busy.' Marco nodded towards a building on the left. 'That is the convention centre, where the film festival is held.'

Isobel glanced over and saw the impressive red-carpeted steps where all the stars had their photos taken, and she remembered suddenly that Marco and Lucinda had been photographed there. Marco had been wearing a tuxedo and Lucinda a long white dress.

She remembered how stunning the actress had looked, and how everyone had commented on the fact that they made such an attractive couple.

She probably should question Marco about it now, but strangely as she looked over at him the words seemed to stick in her throat. She was loath to break the relaxed mood of the day. Or was the reason verging on something deeper…? By Marco's own admission he had been cut up by the divorce— was she worried about delving more for fear that she would find he was still in love with his ex-wife? Because she was starting to get the feeling he was hiding something like that from her.

The knowledge swirled inside her uncomfortably. If she didn't get her act together she was heading for a fall both professionally *and* personally, she told herself furiously.

It would make no difference to her if he were still in love with Lucinda, because her affair with Marco was a two-day interlude at most, she reminded herself sharply. She needed to get her story…needed to have something at the end of their time together.

'You've gone very quiet.' Marco looked over at her.

She shrugged. 'Actually, I was just remembering that you and Lucinda attended the Film Festival together a few years ago.'

'Yes…Lucy was in a film that was nominated for an award.'

The way he said her name sounded warm.

'That was a long time ago,' he said quietly.

Hell, in some ways it felt like a lifetime ago. They'd been happy when they'd been here, he remembered. Happy making plans for the future because Lucinda had just found out she was pregnant…

They stopped at traffic lights. Isobel watched as he adjusted the controls to increase the cold air blowing on them.

There it was again—that grim expression on his face. As if he was remembering something…something that really hurt.

Her heart thudded uncomfortably as she prepared to ask him what had happened. But she just couldn't… The time wasn't right now, she told herself fiercely.

Marco had been expecting her to follow through with the usual questions, but to his surprise she fell silent. He frowned. He really couldn't make up his mind about her at all; just when he thought she was reverting to type she became once more the rather vulnerable young woman who for some reason intrigued him.

'I thought we'd stop and have breakfast out of town. There's a lovely restaurant just a few miles out with great views,' he suggested casually.

She nodded. 'Anyway, the paparazzi will probably be out in force around here, so I suppose a retreat out into the country is a better idea.'

He laughed. 'Yes, there is that.'

Isobel leaned her head back. She wasn't losing sight of reality, she reassured herself. She would ask all the questions she needed to ask later. Why spoil the day by broaching them now? Why not just enjoy these moments with a handsome man?

The Corniche d'Or was one of the most spectacular roads Isobel had even travelled along. The dramatic cliffs were a red-gold colour that seemed to blaze against a backdrop of blue sea and sky and the road snaked around between them, hugging hairpin bends and giving amazing views down over sheer drops to the sea.

Isobel felt a bit dizzy at some parts, and was glad that Marco was such a good driver. A little further on they pulled in at the restaurant Marco had mentioned.

The views over the sea were breathtaking and they lingered on the sunny terrace, drinking coffee and eating *pain au chocolat*, laughing and talking about nothing in particular.

'I would never usually eat chocolate for breakfast,' Isobel told him a little later as they strolled along a white sandy beach. 'I feel a bit like I'm on holiday.'

Marco had to admit for the last few hours he'd felt more relaxed than he had done in a long time.

He smiled, and turned her around so that he could look at her. The breeze was blowing her hair around her shoulders in silken waves, and she looked young and carefree.

'So let's *be* on holiday,' he suggested suddenly. 'Let's call the yacht and sail along the coastline for a few days—making love at lunchtime, eating and drinking, doing *absolutely* what we want.'

The suggestion sent little thrills racing through her.

'And what about work?'

'What about it?' There was a gleam of devilment in his gaze. 'I have a meeting in New York in three days…I can give work a miss until then.'

'And what do I tell my editor? Because she will be asking for an update soon…'

'Turn your phone off,' Marco told her with a grin. 'Or tell her that things just got complicated.'

CHAPTER TEN

THE sun was beating down from an uncompromising clear blue sky, and the temperatures were spiralling into the mid-thirties.

Isobel walked to the rail of the yacht to try and find a cooling sea breeze, but there was hardly a breath of air stirring.

They were anchored out in the bay of St Tropez and, gazing out across the bright silver glitter of the sea, she could see the town nestling at the foot of green hills, with dusky purple mountains rising behind in the distance. The town seemed to sparkle in the sunlight, its terracotta roofs and bell tower like something from an Impressionist painting.

Isobel thought that it was probably the most perfect view, and she tried to store it away in her memory banks so that she could remember it on grey winter days to gladden her heart. She was storing up a lot of perfect memories, she thought with a smile. Because these last few days with Marco had been nothing short of idyllic.

On the first day they had sailed down the coast to Juan-les-Pins, where they had taken lunch and window-shopped around the most exclusive of boutiques.

Later, when Isobel had got back to the yacht, she had found all the clothes and the swimwear she had admired had been delivered to their cabin.

She had been mortified—and still was—but Marco had insisted that she needed a 'holiday wardrobe', and as she had nothing to wear other than the clothes she stood up in, she really hadn't been in a position to argue.

Isobel had never possessed such a wonderful wardrobe: linen dresses that flowed coolly around her body in the heat of the sun, silk evening dresses for dinner on deck, and the most sensuous of underwear and night attire.

For the first time in her life she felt desirable and glamorous... OK, not in the same league as Marco's usual women-friends, but attractive just the same. And that wasn't just down to the clothes Marco had bought for her, but also to the way Marco made her feel. He'd been treating her as if she was special to him—had wined and dined her under the stars, had taken her out for meals and for picnics. They'd visited the island of St Honorat and walked through fields of wild poppies and olive trees, had sipped champagne in the shade of eucalyptus trees. Made love on the deck of the ship in the heat of the day and under the cool blaze of the stars at night.

It had been the most perfect three days of her life, and she didn't want their time together to end. But she knew it had to. Knew that tomorrow Marco had to fly to New York.

They hadn't talked about it, but the knowledge had lain heavily between them ever since they'd got up this morning. She'd tried very hard not to let it spoil their remaining time together, but there was a sadness inside her that was hard to ignore.

Marco was in his office now, taking his first business phone call in three days. And over dinner tonight she was going to have to broach the subject of their interview.

She'd got to know him during their time together, and she would now be able to write about his phenomenal rise to become one of the most successful businessmen of their times, would be able to discuss his wicked sense of humour, his poverty-stricken background in Naples, the fierce sense of pride that had made him want to make his own fortune rather than rely on his mother's family for backing.

But she still didn't know the real reason behind his divorce. All she knew was that when he mentioned Lucinda's name he sometimes looked unbearably sad, and it made a mockery of her previous suspicions that he hadn't cared about his marriage.

They were pulling up anchor, Isobel noticed, and the masts were being hoisted up. Suddenly she wished that Marco was beside her—that he would put his arms around her and tell her that everything was going to be all right, that this wasn't the beginning of the end. But there was no sign of him, and she knew she was being unrealistic—because although they'd shared a wonderful time together there had been no false promises. She knew exactly where she stood.

And this was the end.

When Marco stepped up onto the deck a little while later she was standing at the back of the ship, watching the white frothy wake they left in the water as they forged forward with some speed.

She seemed lost in thought, and whilst she was unaware of his presence he allowed his eyes to move over her, taking in every little detail of her appearance.

The long green halterneck dress that she was wearing was very sexy; it was cut low at the back, showing her honey-gold tan and her long straight spine to perfection. Her hair was twisted up on top of her head, leaving a few tendrils to spill down appealingly onto her shoulder.

Over the last few days he had watched as she had transformed before his eyes into a sophisticated and beautiful woman. Even now when he looked at her he had to do a double-take to remind himself that she was that little mouse journalist.

He moved forward, and she turned and saw him.

'I thought you'd got lost down in that office,' she said with a smile.

'Yes—unfortunately having a few days off has resulted

in an in-box jammed with e-mails and a hundred voicemail messages.'

'I haven't dared turned my phone back on yet,' she admitted with a shrug.

He noticed how she tried to smile, how she looked away from him so that he wouldn't see the spark of sadness in her eyes.

'No regrets, though…hmm?' He put a hand under her chin and turned her so that he could look into her eyes.

'No…no regrets,' she admitted huskily. 'I've enjoyed playing hooky with you.' She made her voice deliberately light. And it was true. She didn't regret a minute of the time they'd had together, and she knew the score.

'Me too…' He leaned closer and kissed her—a long, lingering, passionate kiss that made her melt with desire. 'Unfortunately I've had to move my flight to New York forward, due to a problem in the office over there. Which is the reason we're heading back to my villa now.'

'I see…' She suddenly felt very cold, despite the heat of the day.

'But we've still got tonight. I won't have to leave until about midnight.'

'Well…that's good.' She tried desperately to keep the tremor out of her voice.

For a while his eyes held hers. 'I've bought you a little something.' She hadn't noticed the long narrow box in his hand until he brought it forward with a flourish and handed it to her.

'What is it?' she asked with a frown.

'Well, open it up and see.'

With shaking fingers she did as he asked, and then gasped as she saw the emerald and diamond necklace that lay inside.

'It's beautiful Marco…but I can't possibly accept it.'

'Of course you can.'

She shook her head. 'You've bought me too much already.

I shall be leaving France with a large suitcase when I only arrived with an overnight bag!'

'And your problem is…?'

Her problem was that she would trade everything just for one more day with him, she thought, swallowing hard.

'My problem is that it's too much.'

'Nonsense. It's just a trinket—a token of how much I have valued our time together.'

He reached for the box and took the necklace out to put it on for her. Just the lightest brush of his fingertips made her ache.

'There…perfect.' He stepped back to admire the jewellery. 'I thought the stones would match your eyes and they do.' He smiled. 'You have the most incredible green eyes I have ever seen.'

'And you have the smoothest and most charming lines,' she said archly, and he laughed.

'That's what I like about you, Izzy—you always try to be oh-so-sensible.'

But not always with success, she thought wryly. In fact sometimes she felt monumentally stupid—because right at this moment she was starting to believe that she was falling in love with him, and that would be the most foolish thing ever.

The thought made her heart race with fear and she quickly dismissed the idea. She wasn't that stupid! This had only ever been a fling for Marco—she was so out of his league that she might as well have been from another galaxy.

'And while we are on the subject of being sensible, I have a few loose-end questions for my article.' She tried desperately to make herself sound businesslike.

'Well, we can't have any loose ends,' he said with that roguish gleam in his eyes that she knew so well.

'I mean it, Marco,' she said quickly.

'And so do I.' Marco reached for her and pulled her into

his arms. 'And we'd better tidy all those loose ends away... *later.*'

'Marco...' She tried to be strong, but as usual his touch was too hard to resist and she couldn't pull away.

'You know what I'd like?' he murmured, his hand moving to the tie of her halterneck. 'I'd like to see you wearing nothing other than that necklace.'

When Isobel woke up she was lying in Marco's arms and the cabin was in darkness.

She wondered what time it was, and a rush of panic went through her as she remembered that Marco was leaving to-night. She couldn't believe that she had fallen asleep when they had so little time left together! But their passion had been so intense, their lovemaking so frantic, that it had just wiped her out.

'Marco? Are you awake?' She sat up a little, looking for the clock.

'Yes...relax.' He drew her back down to him and kissed her forehead.

'What time is it? she whispered, cuddling in against him.

'Time I was getting up. I was just trying to gather the energy and the willpower to drag myself away from you.'

'Were you?' She hardly dared to believe that.

He rolled over, pinning her beneath him. 'Yes, I was,' he murmured huskily. 'Something very strange seems to have happened over these last couple of days. I think you have placed some sort of weird spell over me with your journalistic voodoo, because I can't seem to get enough of you.'

She smiled. 'Journalists don't do voodoo.'

'Yes, they do. They also speak with forked tongues.' He kissed her on the lips. 'But, hell...it's some tongue...some voodoo...'

'So why don't you stay and sample some more?'

As soon as the words left her lips she couldn't believe

that she had said them. She told herself to make some sort of joke and withdraw the suggestion, but as their eyes held she realised it was too late for that.

So she took a deep breath and continued. 'It's just a passing thought…but you could always miss your flight and spend one more night with me.'

He moved up onto one elbow, and for a moment she thought he was considering the option, but then he shook his head. 'I can't, *cara*. I have an important deal that needs signing.'

'Yes…of course.' She felt her skin stinging with colour as humiliation washed through her. She shouldn't have asked. What the hell was the matter with her? she asked herself angrily. 'You're right—we've played truant long enough. I have to get back to London.'

For a moment Marco wondered if he was doing the right thing. She really did look very enticing, he thought idly. He would have enjoyed another night with her… But then he reminded himself firmly that he really was behind with work, and really did need to get to New York as soon as possible. And maybe it was for the best that they drew a line under these last few days, because in the short space of time he'd known her she had started to become addictive—and that was never a good thing. He knew himself well enough to know that it wouldn't work. He wasn't cut out for cosy relationships—he'd already proved that to the world.

He looked into her dark green sparkling eyes and remembered how new she was to all of this. He really didn't want to hurt her. 'Izzy, you knew I couldn't make you any promises, and—'

'Marco, I can assure you I don't want any promises.' She pulled away from him, the humiliation inside her intensifying. 'I was just enjoying being in holiday mode—nothing more.'

She was sitting on the side of the bed, putting on a T-shirt.

'Have we got time for a coffee, do you think?' she asked lightly. 'I don't know about you, but I really could use one.'

'Yeah, that would be good.' He switched on the bedside light as she pulled on a pair of white-cropped trousers. She was still wearing the emerald necklace, he noticed, and it glinted with the same depth of fire as her eyes as she glanced over at him.

He wanted to reach for her but he forced himself not to. Instead he made himself get out of bed. 'I'll have a shower and see you up on deck.'

It was a relief to get out of the cabin—to stand on the deck and take deep shuddering breaths of the night air. What was wrong with her? she asked herself fiercely. She knew the score—why was she making a fool of herself by wanting more?

Marco was never going to be serious about her...they were a total mismatch. He went for beautiful models or famous actresses, and he detested journalists.

She wondered if he would have opened up to her more if it hadn't been for her job, and for the first time in her life she wished she did something else...

Trying to pull herself together, she made her way over towards the galley. She noticed they were moored by Marco's villa, and she couldn't help but remember the first night, when she had come running down here in her dressing gown. That seemed like a lifetime ago. She felt like a different person now—and certainly not one driven by her career any more, she thought wryly. In fact she had hardly given her interview a second thought over these last few days.

Surely Marco realised that...didn't he?

But whether he did or not it seemed to have made little difference. The only difference was that when she got back to London without her in-depth story she might find herself out of a job, she told herself angrily. And she really, *really* should care more about that.

There was no one in the galley—in fact, looking around,

it seemed that most of the staff had left the yacht. So Isobel made coffee herself and carried it up on deck.

Marco appeared a few minutes later. He was wearing a dark business suit with a blue shirt, and he looked so handsome she felt her senses flip.

'I bet you haven't really got time for coffee, have you?' she said huskily, noticing how he glanced at his watch as he walked over to join her.

'I do need to be leaving soon.' He took a sip of the drink and then put it down. 'I've arranged for a member of staff to pack your clothes and bring them up to the house for you. I think it would be better if you slept up there tonight.'

He sounded so crisp and businesslike. A million miles away from the way he'd been with her over these last few days. She'd thought she'd been gradually getting closer to him, but that had just been an illusion, she told herself fiercely. This was reality.

'Fine…' She shrugged, not really caring where she spent the night now. 'I'll arrange a flight home first thing tomorrow.'

'I've taken care of that for you. My chauffeur will pick you up at ten.'

'You've thought of everything.'

Everything except how difficult it was to leave her, Marco thought suddenly. With a frown, he glanced again at his watch. 'Come…walk up to the house with me. *cara*.'

He reached and took hold of her hand, and she wanted to pull away from him, to angrily tell him not to touch her. But she didn't…because she just didn't have the willpower.

They walked in silence for a while through the darkness of the gardens, following a winding path up through the lemon trees. She could smell their fresh scent mingling with rosemary and the wild honeysuckle that climbed over the arbour leading to the patio.

'There are some photos in the top drawer of my bureau

in the study,' Marco told her suddenly. 'They might help you with your article, so I want you to take them.'

'OK…what are they of?' she asked curiously.

'There are some wedding snaps of Lucy and I in the Caribbean. We managed to escape the glare of the press, so no one has seen them before. There are also some photos of my parents on their wedding day.' As they reached the top of the path he turned to look at her. 'And just for the record, Izzy, I *did* love Lucy very much.'

'Yes…I kind of gathered that.' She shrugged, and something made her add softly, 'So couldn't you forgive her?'

'Forgive her for what?'

'For…' She paused and wished she could see the expression on his face, but the patio was in darkness and he was standing in the shadow of the trees. 'I assumed she was the one who had an affair…' Isobel shrugged. 'She was an actress, and—'

'And therefore it follows that she had to be unfaithful?' He cut across her fiercely. 'You journalists are all the same, aren't you? Jumping to conclusions to the last.'

'I don't deserve that, Marco!' she snapped. 'I've gone out of my way not to judge—not to ask painful question, and not to intrude! Is that how you think of me? As—as just another journalist?'

The question lingered between them in the darkness, and when he didn't answer immediately she turned away, running up the steps, wanting to get as far away from him as possible.

He caught her by the arm just as she reached the front door.

'Izzy, wait.' He swung her around. 'That's not how I think of you.'

'Well, you could have fooled me. You haven't answered any of my questions about your marriage and I haven't pushed you.'

'It wouldn't have made any difference if you had,' he said

softly. 'I never had any intention of telling you anything about my marriage. At first because you were a journalist, and then because…because we were having too good a time, and I found myself switching off from the past.' He frowned. 'Not something I do very easily, if the truth be told.'

She swallowed hard. 'So what happened, Marco?' she murmured.

Marco was silent for a long time before he finally answered. 'Lucy was pregnant—eight months, to be precise—when she lost our baby.'

'God, Marco—I'm so sorry!' She looked at him in horror. 'Why didn't you tell me? I thought…'

'You thought like everyone else that our break-up had to be about infidelity.' His eyes were harsh as they met hers. 'But you don't have to be unfaithful for a marriage to break apart. Our divorce was about loss—the loss of a baby—and our complete inability to deal with it.'

'I'm so sorry, Marco! I'd no idea! There was never even any hint or rumour about the pregnancy.'

'Yes, well…as you know we both worked very hard to have our privacy. And Lucy had a big part lined up in a movie twelve months down the line. She didn't want any adverse publicity to ruin it for her, so she was waiting to sign the contract before breaking the news. She was small anyway, and carried quite neatly, so it wasn't too hard for her to hide behind loose tops. And as the months went by she didn't go out as much—became quite the homemaker. I think she was even starting to reconsider taking the part when it was offered to her.'

'So what happened?' Isobel murmured as he fell silent.

'What happened was a car crash.' Marco raked a hand through his hair. 'One moment we were driving through the rain, making plans for the future, and the next I was swerving to avoid a vehicle on the wrong side of the road.'

Isobel looked at him in horror.

'The strange thing was we were both unharmed...or so we thought. But I insisted on taking Lucy into the private clinic we were using—just to get her checked out. They thought everything was OK at first, and then she went into labour. Our son was stillborn three hours later. He was beautiful, Isobel...a beautiful little boy who looked so perfect...'

Isobel felt a cold shiver run through her as she saw the bleak expression in Marco's eyes.

'Marco, that's so awful... There's no words to say how—'

'Words don't help, Izzy... Believe me...nothing really helps. Because I will always feel guilty...always.'

'Why?' Isobel frowned. 'It wasn't your fault!'

He shook his head. 'Wasn't it? How do you know that? I was the one who was driving...'

'Marco, you can't think like that! It was just one of life's cruel twists of fate!'

He shook his head. 'Well, we will never really know that for sure, will we? The only thing I do know for sure is that it was the catalyst for our divorce. And I could have handled it better. We were both so devastated, both so driven to do anything to forget, that we started burying ourselves into our work. Things fell apart pretty quickly after that. But there was no affair, Izzy. Sometimes I wish there had been—it might have been easier. We could at least have hated each other.'

'And instead you still love her...?'

She didn't know if Marco didn't hear that question, because her voice was so low, so tremulous, or whether it he didn't want to answer it. But he made no reply, and at that same moment the limousine pulled into the drive behind him.

'That's my lift to the airport. I'd better go.'

She frowned. 'Marco, is this the first time you've talked about this to anyone?'

'Yes...and I picked a journalist...on my own front doorstep!' He looked at her with a raised eyebrow. 'Life can really throw some unexpected curveballs, can't it?'

'You know I won't say anything,' she whispered unsteadily.

'Well, I'm in your hands now, aren't I?' He shrugged. 'Izzy,
I suddenly don't care what you write…just so long as you go
easy on it for Lucy's sake…OK?'

'You don't even need to say that.'

For a moment neither of them moved. They just looked
into each other's eyes.

'You're a pretty special person, *cara*.' He stroked a hand
along the side of her face. 'And if I had to tell anyone about
my marriage, I'm glad it was you.' Then he turned towards
the car and was gone.

Isobel stood where she was until the red lights of the car
disappeared into the darkness.

CHAPTER ELEVEN

'WHAT was Marco Lombardi really like?'

Isobel was starting to wish she hadn't come into the office today. Because if she'd had a pound for every time she'd been asked that she would have been able to fly first-class to the Caribbean tonight—or maybe New York. Not that she *wanted* to go to New York, she told herself categorically. It was just a passing thought.

'He was very charming, as you would expect, Joyce.' She answered the secretary's question cheerfully, and then gave a sigh of relief as the woman nodded her head and seemed to accept the set turn of phrase.

'I thought he would be. I really enjoyed your article about him, by the way. He sounds as if he's a genuinely good man... all those charities that he has supported for years in secret... how lovely is that? And he seems to have been genuinely cut up by his divorce. And of course he's gorgeous; you're *so* lucky to have met him.'

The woman walked away before Isobel had a chance to comment on that. She wasn't so sure about that last observation at all. Sometimes, as she lay alone in her double bed and thought back to those few days with Marco, she wished she had never met him...because she missed him too much. Other times she wouldn't have changed a thing.

It was seven weeks ago now. Of course she hadn't heard

from him, and she didn't expect to. *Nor did she want to*, she reminded herself heatedly, because it was just a fling.

Best to chalk it up as an experience and forget it.

Trouble was, it was hard to forget Marco when everyone kept mentioning him. She had written quite a sensitive piece on him, focusing on his achievements and underlying it with his sense of loss about his marriage break-up. She hadn't mentioned the child he had lost—had just said that pressures of work and the constant intrusion of the press had all contributed to put pressure on his relationship. And then she had talked about his tough upbringing and his early years in Naples.

Everyone had been fascinated as it had shown a totally different side to him—well away from his womanising image. The sales of the paper that weekend had gone through the roof, and her editor had been so pleased that she now wanted Isobel to do another article.

'Let's ring him up and see if we can do an informal "at home with Marco" item,' she'd suggested excitedly earlier that day. 'This time maybe he will allow us to send a photographer with you.'

Isobel had tried to tell her that Marco was a very busy man and probably wouldn't take her call. 'He doesn't like the press,' she'd reiterated over and over. 'He said this was a one-off interview to put an end to all the speculation about him.'

But her editor hadn't wanted to hear that, and she'd been summoned into the office today to discuss it.

Well, she was damned if she was going to contact Marco again, Isobel thought angrily as she gathered her notes together. She'd told her editor that she'd go with what she already knew. Maybe she could write about his house—describe the décor? Or write about his yacht or something? But nothing had been finalised.

As she put everything away into her briefcase Isobel was aware that she hadn't used the photos Marco had given her in

France. Instead she'd gone with old ones from the newspaper's archives for her article.

Which meant that she could have offered them to her editor today and taken some of the pressure off.

But for some reason she hadn't been able to bring herself to do it.

They were too poignant. They opened up all sorts of questions in Isobel's mind about Marco's feelings for his ex-wife.

Did he still love her?

She needed to switch off from the subject—go home and get some rest. Because she was tired—really tired. Probably due to the fact that she hadn't been sleeping too well. Her nights as well as her days seemed to have been haunted by thoughts of Marco Lombardi lately. Well, no more, she told herself firmly.

The rain was bouncing off the pavements outside, and Isobel lingered in the shelter of the lobby for a moment, wondering if she should ring for a taxi.

'Evening, Isobel.' Elaine, one of the receptionists, waved over at her. 'Loved your piece on Marco Lombardi—hell, but that man is good-looking.'

'Yes…isn't he?' Isobel tried to smile. If one more person mentioned Marco to her she thought she would scream—she was glad she'd been doing most of her work from home recently, because she couldn't have stood seven weeks of this.

'Are you writing another article about him? I believe he's back in London at the moment.'

'I think he's still in New York,' Isobel corrected her quickly.

'No, he's back in London. There were pictures of him in one of my gossip magazines a few days ago at JFK—it said he was heading back to London.'

Isobel turned slowly. She hadn't seen anything about that! But then she hadn't been as efficient with things as she usually was. Normally she bought a range of papers and magazines to keep abreast of current affairs, but she'd been feeling so tired that most of them were still unopened back at her flat.

'There are rumours that he will still be here to attend his ex-wife's film premiere. It shows in Leicester Square next month.'

'That will be a good photo opportunity, I wonder if Lucinda's coming over for it.' It took all of Isobel's willpower to try and keep businesslike.

'I don't know—I was going to ask *you* that.' Elaine laughed.

'Afraid I don't know anything more than you. I hardly know the man.' Isobel turned up the collar on her raincoat. She really needed to get out of here.

'Hey, do you want me to ring for a cab for you? It's a horrid night.'

'No, it's OK, Elaine. Some fresh air will do me good.'

Isobel stepped out onto the street. It was a relief to get out of the building and away from the awful, never-ending reminders.

The rain was icy cold, and it was more like winter than summer. She couldn't help comparing it to the warm rain in France. She remembered running hand in hand with Marco through it, laughing with him, kissing him… The memories made tears merge with the rain on her face.

Marco was back in London and he hadn't contacted her. She didn't know why she felt so hurt. It was hardly a surprise. He hadn't phoned her whilst he'd been in the States, so obviously he'd no intention of keeping in contact.

She was drenched by the time she reached the underground station and joined the throngs of people hurrying down the steps. It was the usual Friday night mayhem, and the platforms were packed.

Isobel hated the underground when it was like this. She tried to keep back, so that the crowds didn't hem her in, but as soon as the train pulled in she found herself swept along with everyone else and jammed into a small standing space in one of the compartments. She closed her eyes as the doors closed, and tried to imagine that she was somewhere else.

She only had three stops before she could get off, and usually the visualisation trick helped to make her feel less claustrophobic. Only today all she could visualise was Marco—and that definitely didn't make her feel any better.

Was he here for his ex-wife's premiere? she wondered.

Not that she cared.

The train stopped and more people got on. There was a smell of damp clothing and wet hair. Isobel started to feel a bit queasy.

Maybe next stop she'd get out, she thought frantically. Because she'd rather walk in torrential rain than feel like this.

Come to think of it she'd been feeling a bit queasy on and off all day.

Isobel's eyes snapped open.

In fact she'd been feeling tired and queasy and a bit tearful for a few days.

Weren't they the symptoms of pregnancy?

It was raining so heavily that Marco could hardly see out of the windows of the limousine. He was parked across the road from Isobel's address…and he'd been there for the last twenty minutes.

Where had she got to? he wondered impatiently as he glanced at his wristwatch. She surely should be home by now; the receptionist at her office had told him that he'd only just missed her, and her offices weren't so far away.

He was just wondering if he should come back later when he saw her rounding the corner—her head down against the rain, a bag of shopping in her hand.

'OK, thanks, Henry. I'll ring you when I want you,' he told his chauffeur as he climbed out from the warmth of the car.

Isobel had just opened her front door when Marco reached her side. 'Hello, Izzy.'

The familiar Italian tones made her whirl around in surprise.

'Marco!' She was so surprised that she could only stand and stare at him as the rain lashed down over her. Was he a figment of her imagination? she wondered hazily. 'What are you doing here?'

'Getting as wet as you.' He reached and took the shopping bag from her, noticing how cold her fingers were, how pale her skin was. 'Come on—let's get you inside, out of this.'

Isobel's apartment was on the first floor, and as she went up the stairs ahead of him she still felt as if she was dreaming— that he wasn't really here. It was only when he followed her in through her front door and carried her shopping bag over towards the kitchen that reality seemed to set in.

He was wearing a dark raincoat over the top of his suit, and he looked as incredibly attractive as ever. By comparison she felt like a total mess. Her hair was soaked through, and the grey trousers that she had felt so smart in earlier were sticking to her like a second skin.

'What are you doing here, Marco?' she asked again, her voice sounding strained even to her own ears.

'I thought that was obvious. I've come to see you.' He watched as she peeled off her raincoat and put her briefcase down on the kitchen table. She'd lost weight, he noticed suddenly; in fact she looked quite frail.

Isobel was well aware of that deliberate measured assessment of her figure, and it made her body flare with heat. How dared he look her over as if he owned her? She hadn't heard from him or seen him in weeks, and suddenly here he was, with his bold, sensual attitude... Well, to hell with that.

He didn't own her; in fact he had no claim on her at all—no right to be here at all.

'You know, I'm a bit busy right now. I've got a pile of work to do. So if there isn't something specific that you've dropped by for, I think maybe you should leave.' She tipped her chin up defiantly. OK, he thought he was God's gift to women, and most women would probably have agreed with that, but she was leaving the fan club, she told herself fervently.

Marco smiled. He'd almost forgotten how fiery she was, and how much he enjoyed that about her. 'Well, it's a good job I *have* called about something specific, then,' he told her, his gaze resting on the softness of her lips. Then he reached for her, pulled her into his arms, and kissed her.

Instinctively she kissed him back, her senses pounding in sudden chaos.

'There—that's better,' he said lazily as he let go of her.

She couldn't talk for a moment because she felt so shaken up. She hated the way he could do this, she thought hazily. One moment she was promising herself that she wasn't interested in him, and the next she was feeling hot inside and falling back under his spell.

'You shouldn't have done that,' she told him breathlessly.

'Probably not.' His gaze was still resting on her lips. 'But I'm glad I did. Now, I suggest you run along and get changed out of those wet clothes.'

'Marco, I'm not going to sleep with you.' She raised her chin firmly. 'We had a fling and it's over.' It took all her strength to say the words. 'If you think you can just turn up here and—'

He laughed. '*Cara,* relax—if I wanted to sleep with you we'd be in bed right now.'

'I don't think so!'

He was looking at her in that bold Italian way that made her body start to melt. And suddenly she realised it was probably best not to try and argue that point. Because whatever chemistry had once been between them was definitely still there.

'Go and get changed, Izzy,' he told her again softly.

She hesitated for a moment. Then with a shrug moved away from him towards the bedroom door.

He really had a nerve, turning up here unannounced—and on a Friday night too, she thought as she opened up her wardrobe and rummaged through it for something suitable to wear. She might have had plans of her own…a date.

And serve him right if she had, she thought as she remembered he'd been back in London for a few days. How dared he come waltzing back in here, kissing her as if he had some God-given right to kiss her?

What was he doing here? The question sizzled through her.

And what was she going to put on? She didn't want to look as if she was making too much of an effort for him—but then again she wanted to look her best just to give her confidence a boost.

Her hands shook as she pulled out a plain black dress from the wardrobe.

You couldn't go wrong with a black dress, she told herself reassuringly. You could dress it up or down accordingly. Quickly she took off her wet clothes, dried herself, and then gave her hair a quick blast from her hairdryer.

'Have you eaten yet?' Marco called from the other room. 'We could go out and have a light supper somewhere, if you'd like?'

The invitation gave her butterflies of anticipation. Part of her would have liked to accept. But jumping when Marco clicked his fingers wasn't a good idea. She needed to be sensible. He was already arrogant enough. She didn't want to be some stopgap in his diary.

She took a deep breath. 'No, I've had a busy day—I don't want to go out, Marco.'

Probably just as well, seeing as she still felt queasy. The knowledge swirled inside her, making her nerves increase even more.

She slipped into the black dress and put some lipstick on. That was better, she thought as she gave her reflection a quick check-over in the dressing table mirror. At least she felt human again, and could hold her own with Marco now.

Taking a deep breath, she went back out to face him.

'So, if you don't want to go out, have you got anything in these cupboards that's edible?' He was in the kitchen, assessing the contents of her cupboards, and she didn't think she could have been any more surprised if she'd tried.

She hated to admit it, but he looked good in her kitchen. He'd taken off the jacket of his suit and rolled up his sleeves.

'Marco, what are you doing?' she asked, leaning against the doorframe to watch him.

'I'm raiding your cupboards—because I've just come directly from a meeting and I'm starving.'

'Don't tell me the mighty Marco Lombardi can *cook*?' She looked at him teasingly.

'Of course I can cook. I'm Italian. But I do draw the line at this.' He pulled out a packet of dried pasta from her cupboard and looked at her accusingly. 'What *is* this disgusting stuff?'

She laughed. 'Sorry, Marco, but you're talking to someone who never has much time.'

'Hmm… And someone who has stopped eating, by the looks of it.' He cast a glance over at her. 'You're fading away, Izzy.'

'No, I'm not!' Even as she denied the claim she knew he was right. She had lost a lot of her curves recently.

'Well, we shall just have to put up with this dried pasta…' He was scrutinising her olive oil now.

The oven was on and the kitchen felt cosy. There was

something nice about having him here like this, she thought dreamily.

But that was the crazy part of her talking. She'd liked spending time with Marco in France, and since she'd come back she'd missed him—had felt lonely. But that was most likely because she was ready for a new relationship. A relationship with the right man, she reminded herself firmly. And that wasn't Marco.

She needed to tread very warily.

He was starting to put away her shopping from the bag she'd brought home. *The bag that contained the pregnancy testing kit she'd just bought!*

The memory made her pounce and take the bag from him. 'It's OK—I'll do that!' she told him hastily.

He smiled at her. 'OK—and then you can pour us a glass of wine and watch a master at work.'

'There is no end to your arrogance, is there?' she said with a shake of her head.

'No point being falsely modest, Izzy. It gets you nowhere in life.'

She emptied the shopping and then, when she was sure his back was turned towards her, took the bag with the kit in it into the bathroom.

What would she do if she found she were pregnant?

The question burned through her.

OK, Marco was here now, and this display of domesticity was all very well—but it wasn't real. This situation wasn't real. He was doubtless just here on a whim. And deep down she knew that the last thing he would want was for her to tell him she was pregnant... He wasn't over Lucinda, and he wasn't over the child they had lost.

The reminder made her heart thump uneasily, and she hid the kit at the back of the bathroom cabinet.

She *wasn't* pregnant, she told herself soothingly. She'd had a period since she'd come back from France…hadn't she? The awful thing was she couldn't remember.

She closed the bathroom cabinet and leaned her forehead against the cool of the glass.

Everything would be OK, she told herself firmly.

It had to be.

As Isobel's only table was in the kitchen, they ate in there. Isobel dimmed the overhead light and lit some candles. Then as she sat opposite him she wished she hadn't—because it suddenly felt too intimate.

'So, what are you really doing here, Marco?' She forced herself to ask the question as he reached to pour her a glass of wine.

'I've called to see how you are. Is that really so surprising?' He looked at her with a raised eyebrow. 'We had fun in France, didn't we?'

'Yes, but…that's all it was—a bit of fun. I didn't expect to see you again.'

What she said was true. And he hadn't planned on seeing her again. He didn't want anything serious. But the strange thing was he hadn't been able to get her out of his mind since they'd said goodbye—and that wasn't like him.

He'd tried to tell himself that she was just a journalist, and that very soon he'd probably read about his marriage break-up in detail in the *Daily Banner*—which would make a mockery of those deeply sincere green eyes of hers. But that hadn't happened; instead she'd kept her promise, and her remarks about his marriage had been restrained…even insightful. And that had made him think about her even more. He'd found himself in video conferences, trying to focus on important deals, only to be sidetracked by the memory of her passionate kisses. Or in boardrooms about to clinch a vital deal when he'd remember making love to her on the polished table, their passion so strong, so impatient, he hadn't even been able to think coherently enough to wear protection.

By coming here this evening maybe he was hoping for some sort of closure on all of that.

'Well, I thought we had some unfinished business,' he murmured slowly. 'For one thing I wanted to tell you I read your article.'

'Oh!' She sat up a little straighter in her chair. 'That must be the first time you've ever opened up the *Daily Banner*! I'm honoured.'

'Yes, you are.' He smiled, but his eyes held steadily with hers. 'I don't know what I was expecting, but it wasn't the article I read.'

'Wasn't it?' She looked at him in puzzlement.

'You kept my secret.'

'Did you think I wouldn't?' Her heart thudded painfully.

'I never take anything for granted, Izzy.'

'Especially with a journalist?' She looked over at him with a raised eyebrow.

'OK.' He nodded. 'I should have trusted my instincts more with you. Sometimes I'm too wary. But I appreciate your discretion.'

The words were huskily sincere, but Isobel didn't really want his thanks—and if that was the only reason he'd come then she'd rather he hadn't.

'You don't need to thank me, Marco,' she said quietly. 'But you're welcome anyway.'

'I know I don't need to thank you…I just wanted to.' He looked at her quizzically. 'And something else puzzled me. You didn't print the pictures I said you could take.'

She shrugged uncomfortably. If anyone at the paper found out she had those photos and hadn't volunteered them her name would be damned for all time. 'When it came down to it I didn't need them. You can have them back if you want—I have them safe.'

He took a sip of his wine and let his eyes drift over her thoughtfully, but he made no reply. Something about the way he was looking at her made her senses stir. Hastily she glanced away, trying to remain focused on reality.

'I believe you are going to attend Lucinda's premiere next week?'

'You've been reading the gossip rags,' he accused sardonically.

'Well, actually the receptionist at work has. She told me you'd been back in London a few days and that that was the reason you were here.'

'Amazing, isn't it, how a receptionist somewhere can know so much about my life? More, in fact, than I do.' He shook his head. 'The truth is that I only touched down at Heathrow this morning. We had to stop off in Dublin on the way back from New York, due to some problems with a company I own there.'

'Oh...' Why did she feel pleased? she asked crossly. OK, he'd only just arrived back in the country—but he still hadn't made any attempt to get in contact with her in the weeks since they'd parted. 'And is it true about the premiere?'

'Ah...more complicated. Lucinda has asked me to attend. But it's not the reason I'm here.'

'Let me guess—you had other pressing business to take care of?' she said lightly.

'Yes, some very important business...'

The candlelight flickered between them, throwing his face into shadow. She noticed how his gaze moved towards her lips, and a shiver of need ran through her, twisting into an ache as their eyes held.

How was it that he could make her want him so much that it hurt?

It scared her.

Isobel looked down at the plates in front of them. They'd both finished eating a while ago.

'I should make us some coffee...' She tried to focus on being practical, to snap out of that kind of thinking.

'Izzy...?'

She looked back at him, her eyes shadowed.

'Are you OK?' he asked.

'Of course I'm OK.'

She remembered him asking her that the day they'd sat having lunch in Nice.

She remembered going back to his apartment—remembered how they hadn't even managed to make it into the bedroom in those first few moments because they'd wanted each other so badly.

She pushed the thoughts fiercely away. 'Why wouldn't I be?'

'Just checking.' He shrugged. 'We took a few risks in Nice didn't we...?'

Was that the important business he was talking about? Had he come to make sure there were going to be no unwelcome surprises a few months down the line? She stared at him and wondered what he'd say if she told him she thought she was pregnant. The words hovered on the edge of her lips...

But she wasn't pregnant, she told herself fiercely—and if she was she needed to come to terms with it before she discussed it with him.

'Yes, it was a bit crazy...' She shrugged. 'But you don't need to worry about me—I'm fine.'

She got up to clear their plates away to the sink.

'Maybe you should go, Marco,' she said suddenly.

'Maybe I should.' He stood up and walked over to stand beside her, his eyes moving slowly over her. 'But the thing is I don't want to go.'

'Yes, but it's getting late, and I'm a bit jaded. You know what it's like when you're working hard.' She wished he wouldn't look at her so closely.

'Maybe you should take some time off.' He stroked a hand

absently down over her arm, and it made memories of France stir, made her heart start to race in a way she really wanted to control.

'Well, it's the weekend, so I will.' Their eyes met, and she saw that gleam in his gaze. 'Marco, we shouldn't...' The rest of her words were drowned out as his lips captured hers.

'I know we shouldn't...' He pulled her closer. 'And I told myself that we wouldn't. But, hell, anything that feels so right can't be wrong—can it?'

She tried very hard to be strong. 'Not necessarily true...'

But they were the last coherent words she spoke.

Isobel woke in the early hours of the morning and cuddled closer to Marco's warm body. She loved being with him like this. She pressed her lips against his shoulder and closed her eyes again. Dawn was breaking outside and rain was still pounding against the windows. It might be a good idea just to stay in bed today, she thought groggily. She felt a bit queasy again. In fact she felt *very* queasy. She tried to fight down the feeling, tried to think about something else, but it wouldn't go away.

Hastily she got out of bed and hurried down to the bathroom. She just made it.

It was the first time she'd actually been sick, and she sat on the side of the bath afterwards trying to gather herself together again.

Was she pregnant?

She told herself that she should do the test now, but the thought of it scared her to death.

Just say she was.

Could she go through with it? Could she be a single mother and inflict an absentee father onto her child? And what if she was like her own mother and found it hard to cope?

The painful thoughts made it hard for her to breathe. She needed to do the test. She needed to do it *now*.

CHAPTER TWELVE

Marco rolled over in bed and glanced at the clock on the bedside table. It was six in the morning, and he told himself that he should make a move back to his own apartment. He was playing with fire with Izzy.

He'd been so careful since his divorce about the women he chose to get involved with. He didn't want anyone serious in his life, and he'd made sure that his nights of pleasure had all been with sophisticated and experienced women who knew the score.

Then Izzy had come along, and she'd fitted nowhere into his scheme of things. There was a dangerous kind of magic about her...a magic that had made him forget the rules he'd laid down for himself since his divorce.

He should have called a halt to things when he'd found out that she was a virgin. He glared up at the ceiling. He should have walked away. But he just hadn't been able to resist her.

Just as he hadn't been able to resist coming back to her.

He swore under his breath and threw the bedcovers back. He had to get out of here.

He was almost fully dressed when he realised that Isobel had been gone from the bedroom for a long time. Leaving his shirt unbuttoned, he wandered out into the corridor to look for her.

He half expected to find her making a drink in the kitchen, but she was standing at the window, staring out at the morning.

'Izzy?'

She didn't look around immediately—didn't seem to have heard him.

She was wearing a bright blue dressing gown and she had nothing on her feet.

'You'll catch cold standing there,' he said softly. 'It's not warm in here.'

Isobel wanted to say that catching cold was the least of her worries. She turned and looked at him then, quietly taking in the fact that he was dressed. 'Are you leaving?'

He nodded, and started to button his shirt up as he walked closer to her. 'How come you're up so early?'

She looked about seventeen as she raised her eyes towards his—young and vulnerable, and far too beautiful for any man's peace of mind.

'I couldn't sleep.' She tried to smile. 'What's your excuse?'

'I always wake at six. And I have things to be getting on with.'

'Yes, me too.' Pride came to her defence. She really needed him to go because suddenly she just wanted to cry.

'Hey, you're supposed to be having a lazy weekend.' He put a finger under her chin and tipped her face upwards, so that he could scrutinise her properly.

Her skin was so pale it was almost translucent, and her eyes seemed much too large for her face. 'I think you've been working way too hard over these last few weeks.'

He sounded as if he cared. But of course he didn't, she reminded herself forcefully. 'Maybe I'm more like you than you think.' She found it suddenly hard to keep her voice non-chalant. 'My career tends to come first.'

Marco ran his fingers up along the side of her face, and as he caressed her he could feel her body trembling with reaction.

She wasn't thinking about work now, he thought with satisfaction. And neither was he.

God, he wanted her. Wanted to take her into his arms… take her back to bed.

She was the type of woman who could get under a man's skin very easily, he thought broodingly. Which was exactly the reason why he needed to leave…but weakness was setting in.

Isobel pulled away from him. She couldn't think straight… couldn't function when he touched her and looked at her like that.

And yet this was all just a game to him, she told herself angrily. He could have her right here and now in this kitchen, then go back to his apartment or hotel, or wherever he was staying in London, and just forget about her.

The thought was a sobering shot of reality, and as she stared up at him she found herself trying to imagine his reaction if she told him right now that she was pregnant. There was no doubt in her mind that he would be horrified.

'Anyway, Marco, you really need to go now.' She forced herself to keep her head held high and to sound as if she really meant it. 'I'm going to make myself a drink and turn on my laptop. I like to work early in the morning, when everything is quiet. I'm sure you are the same.'

He looked a bit surprised by her words, and she tried to take comfort from that as she moved past him and flicked on the kettle. It was good to take back a little bit of control. Marco was a man who had too much of his own way where women were concerned.

The last thing she wanted was tea or coffee—but at least it gave her an excuse to turn her back on him. Because if she looked at him she might weaken.

Marco leaned back against the windowsill and watched her for a few moments. He'd told himself he was leaving… but suddenly he was hesitating.

It was as if she'd woven some kind of spell in the air around her.

Well, if he had any sense he'd just get out of here now—because she spelt *danger* with a capital D.

'You're right—I do need to go.' He watched as she took a china cup from the cupboard. She wasn't even looking around at him.

'Just close the door behind you on the way out,' she said lightly.

The cool words made Marco glare at her ramrod straight back.

If he reached out and pulled her back against him she would change her mind—he knew that for a fact! She wanted him as much as he wanted her.

But would it be fair of him to do that when he knew he didn't want a serious relationship with her—*with anyone*?

He only had to think back to that day when he'd got his divorce papers to remember how he felt about commitment.

And Isobel Keyes was different from the women he usually slept with—she would want much more than he could give.

He watched as she made a pretence of opening a packet of tea. 'I do believe the rain has stopped now—if you hurry you won't get wet.'

Marco had been about to walk to the door, but that was his breaking point—because now he found himself catching hold of her arm to turn her firmly around to face him. 'So... no farewell kiss?' He looked at her mockingly.

She seemed almost to flinch away from him. 'Do you mean farewell or goodbye?' she asked softly, and he realised as he looked into her clear green eyes that he should never have gone that far. 'Don't make this any harder, Marco.' She whispered the words pleadingly as she looked up at him. 'Let's just leave things as they are, shall we? Before we irrevocably spoil everything. We both know this isn't going anywhere.'

He frowned. He'd said something like that the last time he'd wanted to finish with someone.

This wasn't right—he was the one who decided.

But he already *had* decided, he reminded himself firmly. As soon as he'd woken up this morning he'd known he should leave.

'OK, *cara*...' His voice held a husky tone. 'If that's how you want things.'

'It is...' She glared at him. 'It really is.'

For a moment his gaze held hers. Then he let go of her arm and nodded.

The door closed behind him quietly.

Isobel could hear his footsteps through the flat, and then the door closing behind him with a resounding thud.

There—she should be glad he'd gone, she told herself angrily.

So why didn't she feel glad? Why did she feel as if the world was caving in on her?

She felt sick again, and suddenly she was rushing for the bathroom.

Marco had reached the front door out onto the street when he stopped. What the hell was he doing? he asked himself suddenly. Did he really want to end things this way?

He remembered how she'd told him that her career came first. But if that were the case she would have told the truth about his divorce, and she would have published those photos he'd let her take from his house.

He remembered how sweetly she had returned his kisses last night, how passionately she had responded to him.

Then he remembered that gleam of hurt in her eyes as she'd turned towards him just now and told him to go—told him that it was for the best.

Somehow he didn't think it *was* for the best. In fact he was unexpectedly sure of it. He suddenly found himself turning around and making his way back upstairs.

Her door was unlocked, and he went back inside and headed through towards the kitchen. But she wasn't there. She was in the bathroom. He could hear her being sick, then the sound of taps running, and then silence.

He paused outside the door. 'Izzy—are you OK?' His voice boomed out in the silence of the apartment.

A stunned kind of stillness greeted the question, and then she whispered gruffly, 'I thought I told you to go away.'

'Are you ill?' He didn't wait for her to reply, but pushed the bathroom door open and strode in. She was sitting on the edge of the bath and she had just rinsed her face, and was drying it with a white bath towel.

'What the hell are you doing, Marco?' She looked up, horrified by his intrusion.

But he didn't pay the slightest bit of attention to her; instead he strode over and crouched down beside her, so that he could see her properly.

'Why didn't you tell me that you were feeling ill?'

The gentle concern in his voice and in the darkness of his gaze was almost her undoing.

'Please, just go away, Marco!'

He reached to touch her, but she flinched from him. 'I don't want you here!' She glared at him. 'I told you to leave.'

'I know what you told me!' He frowned.

'Well, then—go!' She was starting to feel hysterical—especially as he glanced towards the sink and saw the empty box from the pregnancy testing kit.

'Isobel, are you pregnant?' He asked the question in a stunned kind of way, as if he couldn't quite take in what was happening.

She wanted to laugh—except that it wasn't funny. And she couldn't find her voice to answer him—could hardly even look at him.

'Isobel, I asked you a question!' His voice was rigid with anger, and it made her gather herself together.

She raised her eyes to his then, and he could see the truth shimmering in them even before she answered. 'Yes, Marco, I'm pregnant.'

He stared at her for a few minutes, as if not quite digesting the information. 'I asked you last night if there were any... repercussions from our time together, and you said no—'

'I didn't know for sure last night. I'd only just bought the testing kit.'

'So you waited until this morning—found out you were pregnant and then calmly asked me to leave without saying anything!' His eyes seemed to lance through her like daggers they were so sharply furious.

And suddenly she snapped. How dared he be angry with her? How dared he rant and rave like this? 'And what would you have said if I'd told you last night or this morning?' Her eyes blazed into his. 'Would you have said, *Oh, darling, how wonderful. Let's get married and live happily ever after*?' She held up a hand as he looked set to interrupt. 'I was being ironic, by the way—I don't want a proposal. I don't want to marry you.'

'Well, that's OK, then—because I certainly have no intention of proposing.'

Their eyes held angrily for a moment before she hurriedly looked away. 'Well, at least we understand each other.'

'Do we?' He shook his head. 'I still don't understand how you could let me walk out of here this morning without telling me the truth.'

'For heaven's sake, Marco—let's face it: you could hardly wait to get out of here this morning!' She raked a hand unsteadily through her hair. 'And quite frankly I'm in shock. I don't even know how I feel about this...so I'm certainly in no fit state to deal with how *you* feel.'

There was silence for a moment as Marco digested her words. 'I guess we're both in shock.'

'Yes, I guess we are.' She buried her head in her hands.

'We had one moment of carelessness… It's so unfair when people try for months and years sometimes to have a baby.'

The words trickled through him, their reality pulling him up, making him think.

There was silence between them for a long time as he went over and over the situation.

'Maybe we should be looking at this in a different way.'

'What kind of a different way?' She stood up. 'Do you mean like an inconvenience that can be got rid of?' The words tore out of her breathlessly.

'No, I don't mean that.' He caught hold of her arm before she could push past him. 'I was thinking more along the lines of a child being a gift.'

'A gift?' Her voice wobbled precariously on the edge of tears.

'Yes—a gift that is precious…more precious than anything in life.'

As she looked at him she knew he was thinking about his son…probably remembering how he had felt when his wife had told him she was pregnant…remembering how he had felt when their child was lost. Her heart slammed painfully against her chest.

'You need to think very carefully about what you want, Isobel.' He took hold of her hand. 'I can afford to support a child.' He looked at her with a raised eyebrow. 'I can afford to support you both in a more than comfortable lifestyle.'

Why did those words hurt so much? she wondered as she looked into his eyes. Why had her heart lurched with hope just now…? What did she expect? she asked herself fiercely.

'So in other words you think this is a problem that you can just throw money at and it will go away?' She pulled her hands away from his, her eyes shimmering. 'We're talking about a child here, Marco—not a horse that you can shove into stables and forget about.'

'I know that.' His voice was dangerously quiet.

'Do you? Money isn't going to fix this, Marco. A child needs to feel loved and wanted.'

'And you think I'm incapable of loving a child?'

'No—I don't think that!' She stared at him. It was obvious that this pregnancy was stirring up all kinds of memories for him. That he was revisiting the loss of his son. She wanted to say that she thought he wasn't over the death of his child, the break-up of his marriage—*that he was still in love with his ex-wife…*

The words hovered precariously on the edge of her lips, but she didn't let them drop and pushed angrily past him into the lounge. She couldn't say any of those things to him because there was a small part of her that was scared to hear the answer.

'I don't know what I want right now,' she told him unsteadily as he followed her.

'You're thinking of terminating the pregnancy?' He sounded so deeply shocked that she spun to face him.

'No, I'm not saying that! I just…' She bit down on her lip. 'I always promised myself that I wouldn't have a child unless I could bring it into a settled environment. ' Her voice broke slightly. 'My childhood was so chaotic, Marco—I don't want that for my baby.'

She didn't realise she was crying until he came closer—until he reached and wiped the tears from her eyes with a gentle hand.

'I'll look after you, Izzy. I can't say any fairer than that.'

She supposed he couldn't—and she supposed that she should feel grateful.

But she didn't want to feel grateful. Because all she felt was sad and angry. She wanted so much more.

She loved him, she realised helplessly. Like an idiot she had gone and fallen in love with him. Even though she'd known it would never work.

She took a deep shuddering breath. 'I don't want your false promises, Marco—I'd rather be on my own.'

'I'm not giving you any false promises, Izzy. I can't...' He shook his head and then reached for her, pulling her into his arms.

For a moment she allowed herself to be held by him, tried to draw strength from him.

'I can't do the marriage thing again,' he said quietly, almost to himself. 'I have never failed at anything in my life—but I failed at that. So you understand why I will not be repeating the experience?'

'Yes, I understand, Marco.' She raised her head proudly then, and moved back from him. 'And I told you I don't *want* marriage. I don't want anything from you.'

'I'll set you up in a flat here in London,' he said decisively, as if she hadn't spoken.

'I beg your pardon?' Isobel took another step back from him. 'What the hell are you talking about? I *have* a flat! I don't need you or your charity!' She was glaring furiously at him now.

'This has nothing to do with charity! It's practicalities. You can't live here—'

'Marco, I want you to go!' She cut across him furiously. 'I don't want to hear about your practicalities, thank you very much.'

'You're not thinking straight—'

'Yes, I am.' She raised her chin and stared at him calmly. 'In fact I'm suddenly thinking more clearly than I have in weeks. Thank you for your offer, but I will not be accepting your help. I will not be leaving this flat, and I can take care of myself. Now, I want you to go.'

Marco would have argued with her, but for all her fire and determination she suddenly looked exhausted.

'I'll go, Izzy. But only for now. We will discuss this when we are both feeling calmer.'

'There is nothing more to discuss!' she told him heatedly.

'On the contrary—there's everything to discuss. Now, go and get some rest and I'll call you later.'

CHAPTER THIRTEEN

'I THINK your ideas for the follow-up article on Marco are good, Isobel. People will be very interested to read about his lifestyle in France and his lovely home. But you need a little more personal information.'

The more her editor said that to her, the more Isobel felt her blood pressure rising. They had been over and over this a hundred times, and the walls of the small office felt as if they were starting to close in on her. She should have made an excuse to get out of coming in to the newspaper today, she told herself angrily. Because she really wasn't up to discussing Marco.

It was a week since she'd discovered that she was pregnant—a week of feeling as if she was on an emotional roller-coaster. And as time passed the only thing she knew for sure was how much she wanted her baby.

'You really need to contact Marco again and discuss a few things,' Claudia was saying briskly.

She wondered what Claudia would say if she knew the truth—knew that Marco had been on the phone to her several times this week, demanding to see her. The whole situation was tearing her apart. Because she wasn't ready to see him—wasn't strong enough to discuss the situation with him, as he was demanding.

He'd come round to the flat a couple of times too, but she hadn't answered the door. She'd wanted to. And maybe that was the problem—maybe that was why she couldn't face him just yet. Because she was so scared of needing him—scared of being just like her mother, unable to cope without a man by her side no matter how wrong that man was for her. But she *wasn't* like that, she reassured herself fiercely. She didn't need anyone. And she would prove that to herself and to her child.

With determination she reached and took a sip from the glass of water on the desk and tried to concentrate. She really needed to wrap this meeting up.

'I know Marco Lombardi doesn't like the press, Isobel, but you've already managed to get one interview,' Claudia reasoned. 'If you could ring him and get a second that would be wonderful. Perhaps you could even ask him about all these rumours that are flying around regarding his ex-wife's premiere—is he going to be attending with Lucinda, and is there a chance they might get back together? That kind of thing.'

How was she going to extricate herself from this? Isobel wondered frantically. If she didn't agree she might never get out of the office, but she didn't want to cave in. She didn't want to ask those questions.

'I don't think that's a good idea, Claudia. My first interview was closure on the past for…Mr Lombardi.' She carefully avoided using his first name. 'He is totally sick of the press asking questions about him and his ex-wife, and he feels he's answered them now. If I start to ask more questions he'll probably just get so mad he won't even want me to write the piece on his homes.'

'I'm sure you can tread diplomatically around that—' Claudia was distracted by a commotion in the outer office, and she broke off to look out through the partition window.

'Gosh, there is a very good-looking man standing at Rachael's desk, and he's causing quite a stir of excitement amongst the staff,' she observed. Then she frowned. 'How strange! If I didn't know better I'd swear that Marco Lombardi had just walked into the *Daily Banner* offices! That guy is so like him it's uncanny!'

Isobel could feel her heart starting to slam hard against her chest.

Marco would never come here...would he? No, he hated the press, she reasoned calmly. This was the last place he would come. Even so, she leaned forward to look through the window, just to check, and to her utter consternation her eyes connected with Marco's.

'Do you know, I think that *is* Marco Lombardi!' Claudia stood up, her eyes alight with excitement. 'Good heavens, Isobel—how fantastic is this? Quick—ring down to the desk and get the photographers up here. Quick, Isobel!'

But Isobel couldn't move. She was frozen with trepidation as she watched him moving decisively in her direction. What did he want? What was he going to say?

The next moment the door swung open and he strode in. The atmosphere in the room was almost electric.

'Mr Lombardi!' Claudia approached him, and she looked and sounded completely awestruck. 'This is such an unexpected surprise!'

But Marco wasn't looking at her; his dark eyes were riveted on Isobel.

'Well, I was just passing,' he said coolly. 'And I thought I'd call in to see you, Isobel—seeing as you never seem to be in when I call by your apartment.'

Isobel was vaguely aware that Claudia's eyebrows had risen so high they'd almost disappeared into her hairline.

How the hell should she answer that? she wondered furiously. He was going to get her sacked!

So she took a deep breath, tilted her head up, and said the first thing that came into her head. 'Gosh—you've called by the apartment? That was very good of you, Mr Lombardi. I...I just left that message on your answer-machine in the hope we could…eh…talk about a follow-up article. I never expected you to call round in person!'

For a second there was a flare of anger in the darkness of his eyes. 'Well, you should have expected that, Izzy… you really should.'

'Wow—this is absolutely fantastic!' Claudia was fluttering around as if her numbers had just come up on the lottery. 'I didn't know Isobel had already left a message for you! The thing is, we are most eager to do a section on your home in the South of France.'

'Is that so?' Marco grated the words sardonically, his eyes never leaving Isobel's face.

'Yes, we were just discussing it now, as a matter of fact. We were hoping to persuade you to allow us to send some photographers—and Isobel has lots of questions to put to you about your trip to London and your ex-wife's premiere.'

'Well, perhaps I could have a word with your employee alone for a moment, Ms…?' Marco suddenly transferred his attention from Isobel to the other woman and smiled. She practically swooned.

'Miss Jones—but please call me Claudia.'

'Claudia.' He took her hand and shook it. 'I think we might just have some crossed wires here, so if you would give us a moment…?'

'Of course… Take all the time you want. I'll… Um… I'll be outside, in my secretary's office…'

'Lovely.' Marco was opening the door for her, and before Claudia could gather her breath she was on the other side of it.

'What the hell do you think you're playing at?' Isobel asked shakily as soon as they were alone.

'Strange—I was just about to ask you the same question,' he drawled. He regarded her steadily for a few moments, and then took a step closer. 'Why have you been avoiding me when we have important things to talk about?'

'I'm not avoiding you. I told you I needed time to come to terms with…this situation.' She got to her feet and took a step away from him.

'Take all the time you want, but in the meantime we should be working this out together.'

'Look, you don't need to worry about me—'

'Tough. I *am* worried about you—and about my baby. We need to talk.'

'Shh!' Isobel flicked an agitated glance towards the door. 'Keep your voice down, for heaven's sake. Remember where you are!'

'I don't care where I am, Isobel,' he told her calmly.

'Well, you might when tomorrow's paper comes out and our…our business is broadcast all over the country,' she reminded him shakily. 'Marco, I work here! Please… I don't want my life turned upside down by people asking me questions right now—*questions that I really can't answer.* I thought you of all people would understand that.'

'So talk to me now,' he said steadily, his eyes holding hers.

'I can't.'

Her senses felt as if they were in freefall. He was so handsome, so achingly familiar. And he was the person she wanted to open up to most in the world. She wanted to tell him how scared she was—how determined she was to be a good mother and not repeat the mistakes that had been made in her own childhood. How much she wanted this baby… *How much she loved him…*

But there was the problem. He didn't love her. So how could she say any of those things to him? The last thing she wanted was for him to feel obligated to stay around. She'd rather be on her own. She knew she could manage.

She took a deep breath. 'Look, Marco, now isn't the time or the place to talk about this.'

'So get your bag and leave with me, and we'll discuss it over dinner.'

'I can't.' She shook her head and glanced past him to the window. Her work colleagues were all pretending to be busy, but she knew that they were all watching through the glass window. 'Marco, we can't leave here together—think about it. It's going to cause too much of a stir.'

'So what?'

'I told you—I have to work with these people. They are going to want to know every detail of what you're saying to me now as it is. Look, I've got a scan booked in two weeks. Come with me to that, if you want.'

'Date and time?'

The abrupt question flustered her. 'Um…twenty-fifth, at nine-thirty.'

He nodded.

'Now, please just go.' She lowered her voice to a husky whisper. 'I don't want anyone to know about my pregnancy—it's too early. And I can hardly think straight, let alone make any decisions.'

'OK, I'll go—but you've got ten minutes to follow me out to the car.'

'Marco!'

'Ten minutes,' he warned her brusquely. 'Otherwise I shall come back in.'

Without another word he turned and left the room. She watched as Claudia tried to waylay him, without much success, and the next moment her editor was back in the room.

'Wow—what did he say to you, Isobel? Is he going to allow us to send photographers over to his house in France?'

'I'm not quite sure.' Isobel picked up her bag and her coat. 'He said he'd think about it.'

'And did you get a chance to ask about this premiere and his ex-wife?'

'No, not yet. Look Claudia, I have to go. I'll ring you tomorrow.'

It was an effort to get out of the building, and when she did, and saw Marco's stretch limousine waiting for her directly outside, her temperature soared.

'You could have waited around the corner, or something,' she told him in agitation as she got in and sat opposite.

'Nice to see you too,' he said with a smile. 'What took you so long?'

For a moment his gaze moved over her, from the tip of her high heels to the smart black business suit. The look made her go hot inside. 'I...I wasn't long. I was less than ten minutes.'

'Ten minutes and one week.' He fixed her with that steady look that so unnerved her. 'Why are you avoiding me?'

'I'm not avoiding you. I've spoken to you on the phone. I told you that the doctor has confirmed my pregnancy, and I've just told you about my scan. You're up to date. And I really don't appreciate being hauled out of work like this—my job is important to me. I need it.'

'Actually, you don't,' he corrected her softly. 'I told you I'd support you.'

'And I told *you* I don't want that. I want my independence, Marco—I need that too.' She looked away from him as the limousine pulled out into traffic. 'Can't you see that I'm doing us both a favour here?' she whispered the words unsteadily.

'No, I can't see that, Izzy.' He frowned and leaned forward. 'How do you work that out?'

'We don't love each other.' She whispered the words huskily. 'We had a fling and...and this wasn't supposed to happen.'

'No, it wasn't supposed to happen—but it has, and now we need to deal with it.'

The cool, pragmatic words just made the hurt inside of her escalate. 'And I am dealing with it. I'm facing facts. I want this baby, Marco, but you really don't. You're just trying to do the decent thing. And to be honest I'd rather you didn't. Because I know what it's like to have a father who pretends to want you when really he can't wait to get away—'

'Hold on a moment—you think I don't want this child?' He cut across her forcibly.

'I know you don't, Marco. I know you're not over losing your first child and I know how devastated you were—'

'Yes, I was devastated when my son died...and, yes, it's taken me a long time to come to terms with that.' He stared at her. 'But I *want* this baby, Izzy...I want it more than you can ever know.'

The honesty in those words made her eyes start to sting with tears. Furiously she blinked them away before he could see them.

'If you really genuinely feel like that, then I'm sorry... I shouldn't have tried to close you out.'

'Apology accepted—'

'But that doesn't mean I'm going to let you set me up in a flat or anything,' she added hastily. 'I still want to be independent.'

'Well, maybe I was a bit hasty with that suggestion...' He shrugged. 'How about we take it a day at a time from here?'

She nodded. 'But we should be honest with each other. If you're going to get back with your ex-wife then I want you to tell me up-front—'

'Izzy, I'm not going to get back with Lucy.' He reached forward and took hold of her hand. 'Yes, I loved her once— but we've both moved on.'

She wasn't sure how much she believed that. But for now it would have to do, she told herself firmly.

CHAPTER FOURTEEN

ISOBEL turned over the page on her desk calendar and smiled to herself. She was going for her first ultrasound scan today. And she was so excited that she felt like shouting it from the rooftops—she probably would have done too, except that she and Marco had agreed to keep the pregnancy a secret.

For one thing she felt as if it was tempting fate, telling everyone about it too early. And for another she didn't want her photo splashed across every magazine in the land, with all the speculation that would entail. She'd already been snapped by the paparazzi as she'd got out of his limousine that day he'd picked her up from the office, and then again the following week, having dinner with him. But she'd covered it by telling everyone that she was just interviewing him for the follow-up article. And everyone seemed to believe it.

Probably because she was nowhere near as glamorous as his usual girlfriends.

For a moment the notion made her frown, but she pushed it away fiercely. The important thing for now was that their secret was safe—and she didn't have to answer any awkward questions about the future because the truth was she didn't know where her relationship with Marco was going.

They hadn't slept together since the night before she'd discovered she was pregnant, and there was a swirling tension between them all the time. Sometimes Isobel ached for him to take her into his arms... And other times she told herself sensibly that it was best that he didn't. Because she knew that in reality he was only around because she was expecting his baby.

And she suspected that despite his protestations to the contrary he *did* still love Lucinda.

The actress was now in London, for the premiere of her latest film, and she and Marco had been caught on camera having coffee together in Covent Garden yesterday. The press had gone wild with speculation, saying that they were probably going to get back together.

Just thinking about it now filled her with pain. Annoyed with herself, she pushed her chair back from her desk. There was no point sitting here brooding—she needed to get herself ready for her hospital appointment. She'd said she would meet Marco there fifteen minutes before the appointed time.

Isobel had just changed out of her jeans and into a skirt and blouse when the front doorbell rang. For a moment she considered not answering it. She wasn't expecting anyone, and she was busy applying her make-up, but when she didn't go down immediately the bell rang again—loud and insistently.

'All right, all right—keep you hair on,' she muttered as she hurried downstairs and opened the door.

Marco was outside, and just the sight of him in his dark suit made her senses instantly spin into chaos. 'I hope you didn't just run down those stairs?' he enquired lazily, one dark eyebrow raised.

'Well, as you just rang the bell in a very insistent way, what did you expect?' she replied snappily, and he smiled.

'I expect you to think about that child you are carrying and resist rushing around,' he replied, and his gaze moved over her lazily. She looked lovely. Her long dark hair was loose around her face and her skin was radiant, her eyes bright. 'You look really well today, Izzy... No morning sickness?'

'No, it seems to have passed. What are you doing here, Marco?' She glanced at her watch. 'I thought we were meeting at the hospital?' For a moment she wondered if he was here to tell her he wasn't coming—that he had a business meeting to attend or a flight to catch.

She didn't like the cold feeling that thought stirred up inside her, so she raised her head defiantly. 'If you can't come that's perfectly OK,' she added hastily. 'I will be fine on my own.'

Marco noticed the way she held her head, the spark in her eyes. 'Of course I can come,' he said gently. 'I'm here to pick you up.'

'Oh, right…' She shrugged. 'I thought we'd agreed that it was best to meet there because the press might catch us going into the hospital together?'

'No—as you know, Izzy, *you* said that, not me.'

'Did I?' She tried to feign ignorance, knowing full well that he was right—she *had* said that. 'You'd better come in, then. I just need to drink another couple of glasses of water, so that the sonographer can get a good look at Junior.'

'OK.' He smiled at her. There was a part of him that wanted to pull her into his arms, break down that standoffish independent streak of hers… But he held back—just as he had been holding back since he'd discovered she was pregnant. He needed to tread warily, he told himself fiercely as he followed her upstairs and into the kitchen. She was so vulnerable right now. 'You've got ten minutes and then we need to leave.'

He noticed her hand wasn't quite steady as she reached to pick up her glass.

'Nervous?'

'No, not really.' She tried to lie, and then as she caught his eye had to smile and admit, 'Maybe just a bit.'

'It will be OK.'

'Yes, I know that.' She tried to keep her tone blasé. But something about his reassuring tone made her heart twist. 'Let's just get out of here, shall we?'

They didn't talk much on the way to the hospital, and as they walked into the antenatal clinic Isobel felt acutely conscious of the space between them. She wished so much that things were different, that they were a real couple—but that was weak and stupid, she told herself.

She needed to keep strong, and as independent as possible. Because this was obviously how things were going to be from now on—they'd be together for their child but that was it.

The knowledge made the ache inside her grow deeper.

She gave her name at Reception, and couldn't help noticing how the staff smiled at Marco. They all recognised him, of course, and all looked at her with curious eyes.

'Maybe it wasn't such a good idea for you to come here,' she said as they sat down to wait. 'It will probably be all over the papers tomorrow.'

'Do you care?' Marco's eyes held with hers.

'Yes, in some ways I do—because we are going to be bombarded with questions.'

He shrugged. 'Tell everyone to mind their own business.' He smiled at her. 'Like I did with you when we first met.'

She found herself smiling back.

'Ms Keyes?' A door opened and someone called her name, and a few minutes later she was lying on a couch.

This was it, she thought anxiously. Why was she so frightened?

Was it because she'd realised how much this baby meant to her?

She'd always wanted a family—even as a teenager she'd found herself dreaming about the kind of family she wanted. And her dream had always been the same: two girls and a boy, and a husband who adored her…and loved the children so much that he just lived for his family.

She must have watched too many Walt Disney films as a child, she chastised herself angrily. The adoring husband bit wasn't going to happen. She glanced over at Marco's face as he watched the sonographer put jelly on her stomach. He looked stern.

'So, is this your first child?' the woman was asking conversationally.

'Yes…' She looked over at Marco and wondered if he was thinking about his son. She wanted to reach over and take his hand. But she forced herself not to.

'Right—let's have a look.' The woman started to run the probe over her skin. It was a strange, slippery feeling, and the gel was cold. 'You can see your baby now, if you want to look at the screen,' the woman said in soothing tones.

There was silence for a moment, and suddenly the woman was frowning.

'Is everything OK?' Isobel was aware that her voice was strained.

'There's something irregular about the heartbeat.' The woman moved the dials and ran the probe over her stomach again. 'Try not to worry…'

Isobel's eyes met Marco's. Suddenly he reached and took her hand.

'I think I'll just nip out and get a second opinion.' The woman took the probe away. 'I won't be a minute.'

Isobel felt as if her heart was beating so hard in her chest it was going to implode. 'Marco, do you think something is wrong?'

'I think you should try not to get agitated—it's not good for you.' He moved closer.

'You mean it's not good for the baby!'

The minutes ticked by, and they felt like hours…weeks… years.

'I bet you wish you weren't here with me now!'

'Hey, of course I don't.' His eyes met hers again.

'Marco, if I wasn't pregnant you would probably be with your ex-wife right now, making up with her—you wouldn't be with me.'

'Isobel, I want to be with you.'

She shook her head. 'No, you don't. You're still in love with Lucinda...your photo was all over the papers today.'

'Hey, I told you we are still friends. I wanted to tell her about you...she deserved to hear it from me first. You're not starting to believe what you read in the papers, are you?'

'No...' She glared at him. 'Well, maybe!' she admitted reluctantly. 'I'm scared, Marco.' The words were squeezed out of her, her pride deserting her totally. 'I want this baby so much...'

'I know...and it's going to be OK.'

'I'm not so sure! But if the worst does happen at least you won't feel you have to stick around for me any more.' A tear rolled down the pallor of her cheek.

Marco felt the sharp pain of loss as she said those words. He wanted to 'stick around', as she put it. He wanted her so much—wanted to make everything right for her. Dear God, this couldn't happen... They couldn't lose this baby!

He said something in Italian under his breath, then, '*Cara*... you're not going to lose this baby! But if the worst happens I will still be here for you. We will work through this!'

She shook her head, all pretence at being strong gone now.

'*Cara*, I love you...' The words were wrenched from him, and there was an anguished look in the darkness of his eyes. 'I never wanted to feel like this again. I wanted to close myself off from emotions, bury myself in work—and then I met you, and little by little you made your way into my heart, into my soul... Now I feel like you are a part of me. I don't know how it happened. *I didn't want it to happen.* But it has.'

Silence swirled between them, and she wondered if she had imagined those words because she wanted to hear them so much.

'I've been fooling myself where you are concerned,' he continued huskily, 'right from the very beginning...'

'You really love me?' She stared at him, still too stunned to take it in.

'Yes. I was just too…stupid to realise it. Too scared of making another mistake.' He squeezed her hand 'I want this baby, Izzy…but I want you too. I've just been too wary of mucking up your life to tell you. Because I've mucked up before…I'm not a safe bet. And you look at me with such vulnerability in your eyes sometimes that I ache to take it away…to make everything OK… But I'm just so wary of making promises.'

'Marco, I told you I don't need promises,' she told him huskily. 'But I *do* need you to tell me you love me again.'

'I love you with all of my heart, darling Izzy…'

'And if there is something wrong with the baby?' The question tore through her fearfully.

'We'll deal with it together.'

He sounded so sure. Was she going to wake up and find this was all some kind of strange dream? she wondered suddenly.

The door opened and the sonographer came back into the room with a doctor. 'I just need a second opinion on something,' she murmured.

Once more the roller was placed on Isobel's stomach, and everyone was looking at the screen.

'Ah, yes…' The doctor nodded and pointed at the screen. 'You're expecting twins, Ms Keyes,' he said with a smile. 'And everything is looking good.'

Isobel felt dazed as they made their way out of the hospital and across to where Marco had parked the car.

'Did they just say that I'm expecting twins?' she murmured, and Marco laughed.

'Unless we are both suffering from the same defective hearing…yes—twins!'

They got into the car and just sat there for a few moments.

'Twins,' Isobel said again as she looked across at him, a look of wonderment in her eyes. 'And did you just say that you loved me?'

Marco smiled. 'Yes—all true.'

'So it's not some extraordinary dream?'

He shook his head.

'And you are not still in love with your ex-wife?'

'Oh, Izzy, no—most definitely no. We both let go of those feelings a long time ago. Lucy is very happy these days, and so am I—because for the first time ever I believe in second chances…'

Their eyes held.

'I love you, Isobel Keyes.' He said the words softly. 'You will give me that second chance, won't you? You will let me break down those wary barriers of yours and prove that I can be trusted…that I am good husband material?'

'Husband material?' She looked at him with wide eyes. 'I thought you couldn't do that again?'

He reached and stroked her hair back from her face. 'Back in that hospital, when I thought for a moment that we might have lost the baby, I suddenly woke up to the fact that I could lose you too…that you might just walk away. And suddenly taking a risk with love again was nothing…*nothing* compared to the agony of not having you in my life.'

'Are you *sure* this isn't a dream?' she asked shakily.

He shook his head. 'So how about it, Izzy? Will you let me take care of you, protect you…love you for all time?'

She started to cry.

'*Cara*…don't cry. I know you have trust issues, but I promise I won't let you down.'

'Oh, God, Marco—I love you so much.' She went into his arms then, and they kissed, and a kiss had never felt so good… so blissful…like coming home, she thought dreamily.

It wasn't until they broke apart that they realised the car

was surrounded by paparazzi, frantically capturing every minute of their embrace.

'Time to take this somewhere more private, I think,' Marco said as he looked into her eyes. 'Back to my place?'

'That sounds good to me.'

A STORMY SPANISH SUMMER
by Penny Jordan

Duque Vidal y Salvadores hated Fliss Clairemont—but now he must help her claim her inheritance! As their attraction takes hold, can Vidal admit how wrong he's been about her…?

NOT A MARRYING MAN
by Miranda Lee

Billionaire Warwick Kincaid asked Amber Roberts to move in, but then became distant. Is her time up? The chemistry between them remains *white-hot* and Amber finds it hard to believe that her time with Warwick is *really* over…

SECRETS OF THE OASIS
by Abby Green

After giving herself to Sheikh Salman years ago, Jamilah Moreau's wedding fantasies were crushed. Then Salman spirits her off to a desert oasis and Jamilah discovers he still wants her!

THE HEIR FROM NOWHERE
by Trish Morey

Dominic Pirelli's world falls apart with the news that an IVF mix-up means a stranger is carrying his baby! Dominic is determined to keep waif-like Angelina Cameron close, but who will have custody of the Pirelli heir?

On sale from 18th February 2011
Don't miss out!

TAMING THE LAST ST CLAIRE
by Carole Mortimer

Gideon St Claire's life revolves around work, so fun-loving Joey McKinley is the sort of woman he normally avoids! Then an old enemy starts looking for revenge and Gideon's forced to protect Joey—day *and* night…

THE FAR SIDE OF PARADISE
by Robyn Donald

A disastrous engagement left Taryn wary of men, but Cade Peredur stirs feelings she's never known before. However, when Cade's true identity is revealed, will Taryn's paradise fantasy dissolve?

THE PROUD WIFE
by Kate Walker

Marina D'Inzeo is finally ready to divorce her estranged husband Pietro—even a summons to join him in Sicily won't deter her! However, with his wife standing before him, Pietro wonders why he ever let her go!

ONE DESERT NIGHT
by Maggie Cox

Returning to the desert plains of Kabuyadir to sell its famous *Heart of Courage* jewel, Gina Collins is horrified the new sheikh is the man who gave her one earth-shattering night years ago.

On sale from 4th March 2011
Don't miss out!

&RIVA™

Her Not-So-Secret Diary
by Anne Oliver
Sophie's fantasies stayed secret—until her saucy dream was accidentally e-mailed to her sexy boss! But as their steamy nights reach boiling point, Sophie knows she's in a whole heap of trouble...

The Wedding Date
by Ally Blake
Under no circumstances should Hannah's gorgeous boss, Bradley, be considered her wedding date! Now, if only her disobedient legs would do the *sensible* thing and walk away...

Molly Cooper's Dream Date
by Barbara Hannay
House-swapping with London-based Patrick has given Molly the chance to find a perfect English gentleman! Yet she's increasingly curious about Patrick himself—is the Englishman she wants on the other side of the world?

If the Red Slipper Fits...
by Shirley Jump
It's not *unknown* for Caleb Lewis to find a sexy stiletto in his convertible, but Caleb usually has some recollection of how it got there! He's intrigued to meet the woman it belongs to...

On sale from 4th March 2011
Don't miss out!

Available at WHSmith, Tesco, ASDA, Eason and all good bookshops

www.millsandboon.co.uk

Discover Pure Reading Pleasure with

Visit the Mills & Boon website for all the latest in romance

Buy all the latest releases, backlist and eBooks

Find out more about our authors and their books

Join our community and chat to authors and other readers

Free online reads from your favourite authors

Win with our fantastic online competitions

Sign up for our free monthly eNewsletter

Tell us what you think by signing up to our reader panel

Rate and review books with our star system

www.millsandboon.co.uk

 Follow us at twitter.com/millsandboonuk

 Become a fan at facebook.com/romancehq

2 FREE BOOKS
AND A SURPRISE GIFT

We would like to take this opportunity to thank you for reading this Mills & Boon® book by offering you the chance to take TWO more specially selected books from the Modern™ series absolutely FREE! We're also making this offer to introduce you to the benefits of the Mills & Boon® Book Club™—

- **FREE home delivery**
- **FREE gifts and competitions**
- **FREE monthly Newsletter**
- **Exclusive Mills & Boon Book Club offers**
- **Books available before they're in the shops**

Accepting these FREE books and gift places you under no obligation to buy, you may cancel at any time, even after receiving your free books. Simply complete your details below and return the entire page to the address below. You don't even need a stamp!

YES Please send me 2 free Modern books and a surprise gift. I understand that unless you hear from me, I will receive 4 superb new books every month for just £3.30 each, postage and packing free. I am under no obligation to purchase any books and may cancel my subscription at any time. The free books and gift will be mine to keep in any case.

Ms/Mrs/Miss/Mr _____ Initials _____

Surname _____

Address _____

_____ Postcode _____

E-mail _____

Send this whole page to: Mills & Boon Book Club, Free Book Offer, FREEPOST NAT 10298, Richmond, TW9 1BR